PILGRIM STREET

A STORY OF MANCHESTER LIFE

BY

HESBA STRETTON

THE AUTHOR OF "JESSICA'S FIRST PRAYER,"
"BEDE'S CHARITY," AND "LITTLE MEG'S CHILDREN."

ILLUSTRATED BY ALFRED W. BAYES

CURIOSMITH

MINNEAPOLIS

Published by Curiosmith.
P. O. Box 390293, Minneapolis, Minnesota, 55439.
Internet: curiosmith.com.
E-mail: shopkeeper@curiosmith.com.

Previously published by THE RELIGIOUS TRACT SOCIETY in 1867.

Definitions are from *Webster's Revised Unabridged Dictionary,* 1828 and 1913.

ISBN 9781935626671

CONTENTS

PILGRIM STREET

Chapter 1

A BROTHER'S SEARCH

The rain had been falling in driving showers all the morning upon the streets of Manchester, and it was no easy thing to walk along the pavements for the number of open umbrellas which were being carried to and fro by the foot passengers; while it was a matter of some peril and difficulty for a child to cross the slippery streets through the crowd of omnibuses and cabs which were being driven hurriedly about in all directions. Yet if any one had had the leisure and curiosity to gaze about him with such a ceaseless shower falling upon him, he might have seen a child making his way stealthily but swiftly along the crowded causeway, and over the dangerous crossings. A small child, stunted in growth by continual want and neglect, with squalid and tattered rags hanging about him, just sufficient to make it possible for him to appear in the streets. A little scarecrow of undisguised and unsightly poverty was the child; yet his face, in spite of its pinched features, bore a sweet and innocent expression, very different from the aged and vicious aspect of most of his street companions. There was a light in his blue eyes, and an open frankness upon his fair face, with the light hair falling round it, which seldom failed in attracting the compassion and admiration of those persons from whom he ventured to beg, when he felt sure that no policeman was near enough to see him; and he had already learned a wistful way of looking into every face he met, to read there the pity he might hope to find. But upon this rainy morning the child was too busily intent upon some other object to ply his poor trade of begging; and though his naked feet were ankle-deep in mud, and the rain drenched him through his tattered rags, he kept on his way steadily and swiftly, until he found himself in front of one of the chief edifices of the rich city.

It was a very magnificent building, a palace upon which tens of thousands of pounds had been spent with lavish costliness. The squalid child came to a standstill, and seemed to be gazing up at it with a feeling of awe from the broad terrace in front of it, upon which he did not venture to set his bare feet, until he had cast a timid glance at the policemen who guarded each entrance. He slunk under the palisade, and threw back his head to look up at the walls and towers which seemed to rise up almost to the sky, while every window there, and every arched doorway, and the niches in the towers, were decorated with carved woodwork, and colored glass, and chiselled masonry, after a very different fashion of architecture from that of the damp and dark cellar whence he had crept into the daylight. Every point of the building bore some ornament strange to his sight, and the longer he gazed at them the more his feeling of wonder and awe increased. High up overhead, in the very center of the grand front, and at the top of the highest tower, which he could only see with difficulty, there bent over him a great image of a man—or more likely of one of the giants of whom he had felt a vague but chilling fear whenever he had to steal alone through the streets at night; and this image held an immense stone in his hand, as if he would hurl it down from his great height and crush any miserable creature who should venture to enter into the grand portico below.

This doorway, towards which the child cast his wistful eyes, was well guarded by policemen, and could only be gained by ascending a broad staircase of many steps, where there was no possibility of concealment. The boy, disheartened and sorrowful, crept along the terrace with his soundless and cautious footsteps, in search of another entrance, until he came upon a sight which filled him with nameless terror, such as children alone can feel—the image of a fierce and cruel woman, such as he had seen many a time in the wretched street where he dwelt; but under her knee, and in her cruel hands, there was the figure of a murdered child. He stood there spell-bound for a few minutes, and then, with a sob which no one heard, he stole back again, close under the shadow of the grand, massive walls, as far as the perilous flight of steps which led into the inside of the building. All the time he had seen people passing in and out without check or hindrance, many of them of a class with whom he was familiar: women with shawls thrown over their heads instead of bonnets, and men in worn-out clothes, and boots that were little better than the coat of mud which covered his feet; and these were walking up and down the grand staircase with a freedom which at last encouraged the boy. Step by step he ventured slowly upwards, until he found himself sheltered from the pitiless rain within a porch so large that it contained a double row of massive pillars, beyond which were doors of glass; and standing upon tiptoe, the child could peep into the hall within.

Ah! what a place it was! He caught his breath in a deep sigh of amazement and delight. From somewhere there came a beautiful light: yet to him there did not seem to be any windows, unless those were windows which looked like pictures of men dressed in robes of crimson and purple and blue, with crowns of gold upon their heads. The pavement seemed made of precious stones of many colors formed into a beautiful pattern. There were many doors opening into the hall, and a crowd of people were passing in and out busily, very strange people, some poor and miserable, like himself, only none so young, and policemen in their well-known dress, and men in scarlet coats, with long white wands in their hands, and gentlemen in black robes, with white wigs upon their heads. The child, standing upon tiptoe, gazed upon all that was passing before him in profound wonder and bewilderment. A policeman, whose beat was near his cellar, had told him, with wonderful condescension, that the place was called the Assize Courts; but he had no idea of what that name might mean. All that he understood was that somewhere within this magnificent palace his brother Tom was to be taken before the judge, and perhaps would be sent to prison. And whatever would become of him without Tom?

He had some vague hope that if he could creep in unseen by the police, and steal along among the shifting crowd, he might by some chance or other meet with Tom; and if he could do him no good, he could at the least give him the half of a sweet bun which he had begged from a lady at the door of a confectioner's shop as he came along. The eating of the other half had been a great treat to him, and it could not fail to be a comfort to Tom, even if he had to go to jail. But perhaps he would get off somehow, like Will Handforth, who stole an umbrella out of a house when the door was open, and boasted of it among his comrades, but contrived to get off from punishment. And Tom had not stolen anything. If the judge would only let *him* speak, he would be sure to tell him the truth, and then he would know that Tom was not a thief. Perhaps one of the grave-looking gentlemen passing through the grand hall was the judge. Oh, if he could only dare to go in and speak to him! But the child felt that it would be easier to die than to speak to the judge unbidden; and he had no one to speak for him and Tom. He had almost forgotten the grandeur and brilliancy of the place in his profound anxiety about Tom, when he was suddenly startled from his survey by a hand seizing the collar of his ragged jacket, and by being well shaken in the strong, rough grasp of a policeman.

"Now, you be off," he said harshly; "at any rate I'll keep the courts free of such miserable young fry as you."

"Oh, please leave me alone," implored the child, "I only want to see Tom; and perhaps he'll be sent to jail for ever so long, and I shall never see him again."

"He'll not be here," was the answer; "and if you don't take yourself off, I'll kick you off. Crowding up the courts with such beggars as you! Be off, I say."

The boy turned away without another word, and descended slowly, one by one, down the steps of the broad staircase, until he came to the lowest. He was in the pelting rain again now; but the policeman had returned to the shelter of the portico, and was no longer watching him, so he sat down upon the wet stones, and gathered his rags about him as he leaned his head upon the step above him. He had no one in the world but Tom, and Tom was somewhere within these walls; and after a fit of silent weeping, which was both strange and pitiful in a child so young, he fell into an uneasy slumber. The rain washed his naked feet, and drenched his rags through and through, and matted his fair hair, but it did not awake him. The people also passed up and down, men and women and children, but as if by common consent they left the wretched child in peace; until at last he was roused by being gently stirred with a stick, and starting up in a fright with a dream of policemen, he opened his eyes, and saw a face bending over him.

A pleasant face it was, grave but kind, and just now there was a look upon it which in some way made the heart of the miserable child feel light and glad. It was very plain to him that he was

THE CHILD FELL INTO AN UNEASY SLUMBER.

a gentleman, and the boy sprang to his feet, and stroked the front curls of his wet hair by way of making him a suitable salutation.

"What are you doing here, my boy?" he asked.

"I wanted to see Tom," said the child, without any feeling of shyness or terror; "he's somewhere in there, and he's going to be taken before the judge, and perhaps he'll be sent to jail, and I'm afraid of never seeing him again."

"What has Tom been doing?" asked the gentleman.

"Please, sir, Tom hasn't done nothing," answered the child; "only Will Handforth's father and another man broke into a house one night, and there was a boy with them, and the police say it was Tom; and they've taken him to jail, and he's been there three weeks and more. But it wasn't Tom, I'm sure; and oh! I wish there was somebody to tell the judge."

"How do you know Tom did not go with Will Handforth's father?" said the gentleman.

"He was along with me all night," answered the boy, eagerly. "We were selling chips up at Longsight till nigh upon nine o'clock, and Tom came to bed before I was asleep. But in the morning the police came and took Tom away, and Tom, he says to me, 'Phil, it's not true; I shall get out of this.' But he hasn't got out yet, and Will Handforth's mother—that's where we live— says he'll be sent to jail with her husband, whether he's done anything or not."

"Is your name Philip, my boy?" inquired the gentleman.

"It's only Phil," he answered.

"Well, my name is Philip," said the stranger, smiling, "Philip Hope. And what is your other name, my little fellow?"

"I haven't any other," said Phil; "but Tom's other name is Haslam—Tom Haslam he's called."

"Phil," said Mr. Hope, "follow me, and we will try to see Tom."

Chapter 2

GUILTY OR NOT GUILTY?

Mr. Hope ascended the steps of the Assize Courts, closely followed by Phil, who shrank with dread from the severe eye of the first policeman whom they met. He was a tall, strong man, stiff and straight as an arrow, with a rigid face that could not readily be moved either to a smile or a frown. He was about to lay his hand upon little Phil, as he ventured to enter the grand hall under the protection of his new friend, when he was arrested by Mr. Hope speaking to him.

"Banner," he said, "can you tell me anything of the case of Handforth and others on the charge of housebreaking?"

"To be sure I can," answered Banner; "the house is in my beat, sir, but I was off duty at the time. Two men and a boy engaged in it; the men were taken in the house, but the boy escaped. They're up now, sir, before Mr. Justice Roberts."

"This little fellow says his brother was at home all night with him," said Mr. Hope. "Is not the boy's name Tom Haslam?"

"Ay, sir, Tom Haslam," replied Banner, "that's the lad's name. But it's no use hearkening to these young ones; it's only encouraging them in their lies. They are born and bred liars and thieves, sir."

The gentleman sighed, and looked down upon Phil with

such an expression of pity and tenderness, that the child was emboldened to speak, even in the presence of the policeman.

"It isn't a lie," he said, thrusting his little hand into Mr. Hope's, and looking up with new-born confidence; "there's Nat Pendlebury and Alice could tell if somebody 'ud only ask them. They know that Tom was with me. Oh! whatever can I do if Tom is taken to jail again?"

"Banner, I will inquire into this," said Mr. Hope. "Do you say the prisoners are before Justice Roberts?"

"Ay, sir; this way, if you please," answered Banner, striding away towards a corridor leading to the interior of the building. But Mr. Hope bade him and Phil wait for a few minutes, which the child did in fear and trembling, and without so much as moving one of his restless little feet under the stern gaze of Banner. Before long he heard the voice of his friend again, but he could scarcely believe it was the same, as he appeared in a black robe, and with a grey wig above his dark hair. Mr. Hope smiled, and again bade him follow in his steps, and conducted by Banner, they went a few paces down the arched corridor, and turned into a room filled with people.

It was not the great Criminal Court, as large as many a church and chapel, with galleries in it for the accommodation of those persons who wished to be present at the trials; the number of prisoners was large, and this was an additional court, held in a smaller room, in order that the business of the Assizes might be more quickly despatched. But to Phil the place seemed large, and crowded with strange faces until Mr. Hope told Banner to lift him on to a bench, and bade him look round if he could see Tom. It was a minute or two before he looked in the right direction; but at length he saw a clear spot near the middle of the room, railed round and separated from the rest, where stood Handforth and another man, and beyond them Tom, with his black hair and eyes, and his familiar face, only more dogged and downcast than Phil had ever seen it before. Somebody was just crying out in a loud voice, "Thomas Haslam!" and Tom looked up for a moment, and moved his lips, but Phil could not hear any sound come from them. Other words were said which Phil could not understand, and Handforth and the other man answered, "Guilty," in a loud, bold voice; and then Tom uttered something, and Banner laid his hand heavily on Phil's shoulder.

"Eh!" he said, "he pleads guilty. He says he did it, and he'll be sent to jail for it, and serve him right, the young rascal!"

For a moment Phil could not understand it; but as soon as the thought of Tom going away from him into jail broke upon his mind, a childish cry ran through the quiet court, and the judge looked round, and a hard voice called "Silence! silence!" But Phil heard and saw nothing but Tom and the judge.

"Oh, Judge!" he cried, "Tom didn't do it. He was at home with me all night, and Nat Pendlebury and Alice know he was."

It was a clear, shrill little voice, and not a word was lost in the silence. Tom started, and looked round eagerly, and the dogged expression passed away from his face as he caught sight of Phil standing on the bench, with his thin small arms, so plainly seen through his ragged jacket, stretched out towards him. Mr. Hope was speaking in a low tone to the judge; and the judge fastened his eyes keenly and penetratingly upon Tom.

"Thomas Haslam," he said, "Mr. Hope undertakes your cause. I will try another case before this. Let the prisoners at the bar be removed."

In a few minutes more Phil found himself in a small, detached room with Banner and Mr. Hope and Tom. Tom's hand was firmly clasped between both his own, and they were standing together before Mr. Hope, with Banner behind them, ready to seize Tom, and carry him back to jail, if he were proved guilty. Tom's black eyes were searching Mr. Hope's face with a keen and cautious scrutiny, but after the search was ended, and he had looked fully into Mr. Hope's own kindly eyes, the lines of his face grew less hard, and there was something like a smile playing round his hungry mouth.

"My boy," said Mr. Hope, "are you or Phil telling the truth?"

"Phil," answered Tom, pressing the child's hand fondly.

"What were you going to plead guilty for?" asked Mr. Hope.

"It were no good to say I were 'Not guilty,'" said Tom, a surly look returning to his face. "The police swore I were guilty, and the others were going to say they were guilty; and they said the judge would be ten times harder on me if I said I were not guilty; so that was how I came to say I were guilty. The judge knows nought about poor folks like me."

"You do not care much about telling the truth always," said Mr. Hope.

"No," answered Tom, not boldly but frankly; "it doesn't pay for a poor boy like me to tell the truth every time he speaks."

"But now, Tom," said Mr. Hope, "I intend to be your friend, on condition that you tell me the whole truth, and the simple truth. If you have really not been helping in this robbery, I can save you from going to jail. Tell me all you know about it; what you have had to do with Handforth, and what you were doing that night."

Once more Tom's keen eyes scanned the face of his new friend; and then he drew himself up and raised his head with an air of resolution, and began to speak quietly and deliberately.

"We lodge with Handforths, Phil and me," he said; "they live in a cellar, and we have the place under the steps to sleep in. The night they say I was helping in the robbery, Phil and me were up at Longsight, selling chips, and we didn't get home till after nine o'clock, and Phil went straight off to bed because he was cold and hungry; and I didn't do anything but just run to Pilgrim Street, to Nat Pendlebury's, with a penn'orth of chips for Alice. It was striking ten by the old church clock as I came back, and Nat knows it. But before it was light in the morning, the police came and took me up, and said I'd had a hand in breaking into a house the night before."

"Do you know anything about it, Banner?" asked Mr. Hope.

"If what Thomas Haslam now says is true," answered Banner, "he can have nought to do with the housebreaking. It was done somewhere between nine and ten of the night, being a house locked up and left, while the owners were out for the evening. The policeman on duty detected a light in the windows, and knowing the owners were out, he got help and secured the two men, but a lad escaped them by jumping through a back window. He carried off some silver spoons, and one of them was found amongst the straw where Thomas Haslam was sleeping."

"The lad would hardly have carried his stolen booty to his own bed," said Mr. Hope, thoughtfully. "Tom, why did you not speak of Nat Pendlebury and Alice at once, when you were taken up?"

"It were of no good," said Tom, rather sadly; "the police said I'd done it, and the magistrate said I'd done it, and nobody 'ud hearken to me. But if you'd send for Nat Pendlebury, he'll tell you I say true. He lives in Pilgrim Street, and Phil'll run and fetch him."

"Banner shall go," said Mr. Hope; "and Phil can show him the way."

In a few minutes Phil was pattering through the mud at the side of the tall policeman, to whose strides he had to take two or three of his own short steps. Something of the sternness had vanished from the cold eyes of Banner, and he looked a little less severely upon the tattered child, who ran in eager and panting haste at his heels. Two or three times he loitered at the edge of a crowd, more to give Phil time to recover his breath than to seek for an opportunity to exercise his authority. In due time they reached Pilgrim Street, a short and narrow street of poor houses, with no thoroughfare through it, and with cellar shops and dwellings on each side of it, into which the daylight, never very bright in the rooms above, scarcely penetrated. A small, spare man, with a rosy and wrinkled face, and grey, wiry hair, was just turning into Pilgrim Street before them with a bundle of many-colored papers under his arm, and a paste-pot and paste-brush in his hand. The door of one of the cellar kitchens was open, and a girl about the same age as Tom Haslam stood at it, looking out with a smile of welcome upon her face. Phil clapped his hands with a shout of delight, and running on before the policeman, he cried, "That's Nat Pendlebury and Alice!"

Chapter 3

THE BILL-STICKER'S TESTIMONY

E very inhabitant of Pilgrim Street turned out of doors, or gazed from the windows, as Banner paced slowly up the middle. It was one of the more respectable of the poor streets, and the visit of a policeman was rare enough to excite some curiosity among the inmates. The bill-sticker, Nat Pendlebury, turned round hastily at hearing his name so loudly proclaimed by little Phil, and Alice came out a step or two from the door. But there was something more than astonishment in Nat's face, when Banner informed him that he and Alice must go with him at once to the Assize Courts. He turned into his house, followed by Phil and Banner, and closing the door behind them, he looked from one to another in utter bewilderment; while Alice, with a brave face, grave though it was, laced her clogs upon her feet, and throwing a shawl over her head, said she was quite ready to go with her father and the policeman.

"But what is it for?" asked Nat, staring hard at Banner. "I'm a honest, hard-working man, and have had no dealings with the police, thank God for it; and I ask you what you are haling us off to the Assizes for? And Alice too!"

"It's no hurt to yourselves," said Banner. "I've nought against you, man, but there's a lad, Thomas Haslam, by name, up for housebreaking, and he's summoned you to prove an *alibi*. That's where it is. He says you and Alice know where he was on the night of the robbery. You walk on first, Mr. Pendlebury, and Alice and me will follow you. Witnesses had best not talk to one another."

The streets were more thronged than earlier in the day, and the rain was falling still more heavily as Nat walked on before the others, deeply pondering over what he knew of Tom Haslam and his affairs, and now and then muttering to himself a short prayer that God would teach him what to say before the judge. He felt more troubled for Alice than himself; but whenever he glanced back, she nodded and smiled to him, and once she raised her eyes to the gloomy skies overhead, as if she too were praying in her own heart to God. So Nat went on, and gradually fell into the quick short trot which had become habitual to him as he hurried from place to place with his paste-pot and bills, until he reached the entrance of the Courts, and had to wait for the rest to come up, before he could go on into the presence of Mr. Hope. It was not long before Banner brought Mr. Hope into the room where they were waiting for him, but the clouds had rolled quite away from Nat's face, and a perfect calmness was resting upon it. Alice was at his side, and Phil pressed eagerly forward to the front, and listened as if his life depended upon their testimony.

"I want you to tell me all you know about Tom Haslam's doings this day three weeks ago," said Mr. Hope, in a manner which set Nat's heart at rest completely.

"And I'll tell you true, sir, God helping me," answered Nat. "It was the last time either Alice or me set eyes on Tom, or on little Phil, for the matter of that. Many's the time since Alice has said to me, 'Father, what do you think has come to poor little Phil?' This day three weeks ago it was quite dark, sir, late at night, and the children were gone to bed—I've five besides Alice—and she and me were sitting in the firelight, talking afore she went to bed—for I've lost my wife, and there's a many things to talk over and settle where there's a large family—and then comes a single knock at the door, and when I opened it, there was Tom Haslam with a penn'orth of chips Alice had ordered of him. She had just lit the candle, and opened her Bible—I can't read myself, but Alice is a beautiful scholar—and I says, 'Tom, come in, and sit thee down by the fire, while Alice reads us a chapter!' and he said he'd be very thankful, for he was cold and tired. So he came in, and Alice read her chapter, and he sits gap- ing and staring with his eyes and mouth wide open, and I fell a-talking to him, quite unthinking; and bless you, sir, I found he was no better than a heathen we send missionaries to. He didn't know who Jesus was, nor nothing about him, and he only knew God's name to swear and curse by. He'd never said any prayers in his life, and didn't understand what they was. And as for going to church or chapel, it never entered his head. I can't tell you how sorry me and Alice were for him. So I walked along home with him to the very door, talking all the way; and I've never seen him since. We reckoned he was tired of my preach- ment; not that I can preach any more than I can read, sir, but my tongue runs on, when I am speaking about Him."

"About whom?" asked Mr. Hope.

"About the Lord Jesus," said Nat, in a lower tone. "It's like those two disciples who said, 'Didn't our hearts burn within us?' I hope I don't give you any offence, sir?"

"Not at all, my good fellow," answered Mr. Hope, heartily; "but how do you know that all this happened this day three weeks since?"

"This is a Wednesday, isn't it, sir?" said Nat, with a bright face; "that's our preaching night, and Alice and the two boys went with me to the service; and a neighbor of ours was there too, Mrs. Saunders, who has a tripe-shop, and she said Alice might have a jug of tripe for the fetching. No fear of Alice not fetching it! So when I saw Tom so quiet over the reading, I said to Alice, hadn't she a bit of tripe left? It was a sight to see that lad devour it up, for all the world as if he were clemmed[1] to death. I couldn't make any mistake in the night, because we haven't had any tripe since, and Mrs. Saunders sprained her ankle the next day, and hasn't been out since. And trade hasn't been so good with me that we could afford to buy tripe."

There was a smile upon Mr. Hope's face, but Banner frowned severely upon this trifling. If he could have had his way, he would have put Nat through a sharp examination of close questioning, and tied him down strictly to the subject of Tom Haslam's guilt or innocence.

"What time was it when you left Tom?" asked Mr. Hope.

"It struck ten by the old church clock as I got back to Pilgrim Street," replied Nat; "and I couldn't have been more nor five minutes, for I can get over the ground sharper than most men, sir. You get into the way of it when you've a good many bills to post up. Mother used to tell us not to let the grass grow under our feet; but there's no grass in Manchester. We bill-stickers don't scrape the mud off the flag-stones, we're so swift."

"And what have you to tell me, Alice?" said Mr. Hope.

"It is just as father says," answered Alice, modestly; "only we haven't seen Tom since, nor little Phil. I suppose poor Tom was taken to jail; but, Phil, why didn't you come along, and tell me all about it?"

The child started with sudden terror, and glanced around him with a white face, while he shrank towards Alice, and grasped her arm with both his small hands.

"Oh!" he cried, "what shall I do? She said she'd break every bone in my body, and flog me to death, if I stirred out of the

1 Clemmed—to be starved or famished.

house while Tom was away; only I was afraid I should never see
Tom again. I couldn't come to tell you, Alice. Oh! I daren't never
go back again! What must I do?"

"Thee shall come home with us, little Phil," said Nat, con-
solingly. "Alice'll find room for thee somewhere along with the
children. There are only five of them besides Alice, and we'll be
bound to find room for thee."

Alice looked thoughtful for a minute or two, and then nodded her head several times in a manner which betokened that
she had arranged the matter satisfactorily to herself; only she said
in a contemplative tone, which brought a smile to Mr. Hope's
face, "You'll have to be well washed, little Phil."

"You may go home then now," said Mr. Hope. "Tom's case
will not be tried before tomorrow morning, and you will have
to give your evidence before the court then. I have no doubt
whatever that Tom will get off. Banner, show them the way out,
and return to me here."

Nat bowed and Alice curtseyed with deep reverence, and
then, with Phil between them, they started homewards. Banner returned to Mr. Hope, and put himself into an attitude of
attention, and for a few minutes no word was spoken by either
of them.

"Banner," said Mr. Hope at last, "I scarcely understand why
the boy's defence was not taken at the time he was taken up
before the magistrates."

"Why, sir," answered Banner, "the police swore to him, and
so did the other prisoners; and if it wasn't him, it's pretty certain
it was Handforth's own son. Thomas Haslam would be pretty
smartly shut up if he did try to make any defence. Them boys
are born liars, and we never take any notice of what they say."

"They are in a hard case," said Mr. Hope, sighing. "Banner,
you are a Christian man?"

"Yes, sir," answered the policeman, in a somewhat doubtful tone, "I hope I am. I go to church regularly, though it's heavy duty at times, sir; but I do my best at it. I'm not over and above of a Christian, but I'm better than a good many of the force. Our service isn't a first-rate one for religion, sir."

"You can serve God as well in the police force as your clergy-man does in his parish," said Mr. Hope. "Banner, it is of little consequence what our work is; the question is how we do it, and why we do it. Our Master himself was a poor village workman the greater part of his life on earth. And now here is a bit of Christ's work for you to do, Banner. God not only sent his only begotten Son into the world to save the world, but he sends all his sons—every one who has been saved from his own sins—to help to save others. You look after this poor lad a little when he is set free and save him as far as you can. I will have some talk with him myself tomorrow; but you know I shall be going away as soon as the Assizes are over. We cannot take these lads out of the streets, but we can try to make them very different from what they are. Banner, will you do your best for this boy?"

"Yes, sir," answered Banner; "I'll keep a sharp lookout upon him, you may depend upon me."

"But, Banner," continued Mr. Hope, "if you are to do this lad any good, you must try to love him. Nay, you *must* love him. Christ could have saved none of us if he had not first loved us."

Banner looked grave and perplexed. It was an unheard-of thing to ask a policeman to feel any affection for one of the mis-erable, thievish lads who were the daily plague of his life. It was not possible that Mr. Hope understood what he was asking him to do. But there was a look in Mr. Hope's eyes, and a compas-sionate anxiety upon his face, which Banner could not disap-point. He lifted his hand to his throat to loosen the stiff stock which almost choked him, and answered, in a husky voice, "I'll do my best, sir. I'm a better policeman, may be, than a Christian, but I'll do my best for Thomas Haslam."

And Banner honestly resolved to do it in the sight of God. He was a man and constable of inflexible integrity, but stern and unbending. He had learned "the *fear* of the Lord, which is the beginning of wisdom,"[1] but he had not gone on to the *love* of God, which is the fulfilling of the law, and the highest wisdom. He feared the judge; he served the king; but he had yet to love and trust the Father, who had revealed himself in His Son.

---

1 Proverbs 9:10.

Chapter 4

WHO IS YOUR FATHER?

The first prisoners brought to the bar the next morning were Handforth and his accomplice, and Tom. The two first pleaded "Guilty" as before; but Tom's voice, which rang clearly and hopefully through the court, cried "Not guilty!" He had caught sight of Nat Pendlebury and Alice and little Phil, waiting near to the witness-box, and for the first few minutes his heart beat gladly at the thought of soon joining them and being free again. Nat gave his evidence in an honest, simple, and straightforward manner, which at once gained the belief of both judge and jury, and Alice confirmed his testimony with quiet and gentle composure. They had brought with them a neighbor who had seen Tom leave Pilgrim Street in company with Nat Pendlebury, and the three witnesses satisfactorily proved his innocence of any share in the house-breaking. The jury did not ask to leave the court, but gave their verdict to acquit Tom in a very few minutes; and the judge pronounced the words which set him free, at the same time warning him solemnly of the danger of bad companionship. Nat and Alice listened earnestly to the judge, and then they left the court, and Nat went to his daily work, while Alice and Phil waited in the grand entrance hall for Tom to come to them.

Phil had been well washed, as Alice had said, and his fair curls shone in the bright light of the morning; for the clouds had been blown away to the west during the night, and the sunshine was streaming down upon the tessellated[1] pavement through the colored windows. The child's heart was full of quiet happiness, and his face, small and thin though it was, with hollow cheeks and starved mouth, looked bright with gladness as he held fast by Alice's hand, and kept watching for Tom's appearance. A lady who was passing by glanced at him, half smiling and half sighing, and was about to stop to speak to him, but a carriage was waiting for her on the broad terrace below, and she had only time to slip a sixpence into his hand and pass on, looking back upon his surprise with a pleased but pitiful smile upon her face.

But Tom was a long time in coming. When he was removed from the bar, and told that he was at liberty to go where he pleased, he was about to hurry off to Alice and Phil, when Banner tapped him on the shoulder, and bade him follow him to speak to Mr. Hope. There could be no disobedience to a policeman's order; but Tom followed Banner with heavy and reluctant feet, as he conducted him along the beautiful corridors to a room of great grandeur. It was a large room, with arched casements and deep recesses, and at first sight it seemed as if it were empty; but Banner marched boldly forward over a carpet upon which even Tom's thick boots made no sound, until they reached the upper end, where they found Mr. Hope sitting at a table with several books before him. He looked pleasantly at Tom as he stood with mingled dread and boldness at the end of the table, and he told Banner to leave them alone, and wait at the door until he had had some talk with the boy. Tom felt frightened, and looked round the room uneasily.

1 Tessellated—checkered as mosaic work.

"Tom," said Mr. Hope, heartily, "I'm right glad we have got you off this time."

"Yes, sir," answered Tom, and for once in his life the tears started to his eyes, he could not tell why; "it's you that's done it, sir. I haven't got anything to pay, sir; and I haven't got any friends, save little Phil. But if ever I'm had up again, sir, and I can pay, I'll be sure to do it. And if there's anything I can do now ———"

Tom stopped, for what could he do for a gentleman like Mr. Hope? a gentleman who was sure to have many servants and friends. No; there was nothing in the world he could do for him.

"I hope you will never be had up again, Tom," said Mr. Hope, gravely. "But there is something you shall do for me, and I will tell you what it is by-and-bye. Now you must answer some questions first. Have you no father or mother?"

"As good as none," said Tom, his face flushing into deep red. "Father and mother were sent to jail when I was about as old as little Phil—that's nigh upon seven years ago now; and mother died before the first twelve months was up, and father has three years to be in jail yet. It wasn't much good getting me off this time, I'm bound to go sooner or later."

"Nothing of the sort," answered Mr. Hope; "you are bound to be something better than a thief, Tom. Don't be afraid to tell me the truth, my boy. Did you ever steal anything?"

Tom hesitated before he spoke again, and gazed earnestly into the face of his friend; and his head sank a little as if he were ashamed to make his confession.

"Yes, sir," he said, "I didn't want to do it, and I was afraid of the police finding me out, and parting me from poor little Phil. He was only a year old when mother went to jail, and I'd the care of him, so that we could not bear being parted. Poor little lad! It's been harder work to get along anyhow than you gentle folks can tell; 'specially since grandmother died, two years ago. I've tried matches, and chips, and rags, and tumbling by the 'buses; but there's been times when I was forced to steal a little for Phil and me. I wasn't ever found out; but I'm afeared I shall be some day, and be put into the jail along with father; I'd rather drown myself than have to live with father; you don't know what he's like. Do you think I should have been put along with father in the jail, sir?"

There was an expression of the deepest anxiety, mingled with a terrible dread, in the boy's manner, as he gazed earnestly into Mr. Hope's face for an answer.

"You would not have been put with your father," he said. "Was that what you were most afraid of?"

"Ay," answered Tom, with a deep sigh; "but for that, and leaving little Phil, I should like to go to jail. You've a bed there, and plenty to eat. And they teach you to read. It's not bad, being in jail, to such a one as me, sir. I'd like to learn to read as well as Alice Pendlebury. Did you ever hear of a book all about God, and somebody called Jesus? It's a strange book."

"It is a strange book," repeated Mr. Hope, thoughtfully.

"Alice were reading out of it that night I was took up," continued Tom, all his alarm and shyness vanishing; "I never heard tell of it till then; and I can't remember much of it, only it sounded strange. And I shouldn't mind going to jail, and learning to read, save for little Phil, and for fear of being put with father. I wish father was dead."

Tom spoke earnestly and simply, as if he were giving utterance to the deepest wish of his heart; but Mr. Hope did not reply for some minutes. He leaned his head upon his hand, and seemed to be thinking within himself, until Tom grew alarmed, and looked hard at the distant door, as if he would have made a run, and have escaped through it, but for Mr. Banner on the other side.

"Tom," said Mr. Hope, looking up at last, "suppose I should tell you that instead of that father of yours who is in jail, you had another Father, who was caring for you every minute, who is richer, and greater, and better than any king in the world, what would you say?"

"It isn't true," answered Tom, with a short laugh. "I haven't got any father but him in jail. Everybody knows that as knows aught about me and little Phil."

"But it is true," said Mr. Hope, "that strange book tells us so. You are worse off than if you had no father, you think. But we have another Father—God, who is our Father—yours and mine, Tom. Every day he gives us food, and forgives us our sins, and keeps us, and delivers us from evil. You don't understand it yet, my boy; but God loves you, and he will make you fit to go to His own home in heaven, if you will try to love Him in return."

"I don't know anything about it," said Tom. "I haven't got any one to love me, save little Phil. How do you know that God loves us?"

"It is written in that strange book that Alice read," answered Mr. Hope, earnestly; "none of us could have known it, or found it out for ourselves, but God sent His Son into the world—the Lord Jesus Christ—who became a man just like us, Tom, only he never sinned and Jesus said that as many as believed on Him to them He gave the right to become the sons of God.[1] Jesus told us also to call God our heavenly Father. We could never have found this out for ourselves; we could never have called God our Father but for Jesus Christ. Should you have known that you could have become one of the sons of God, Tom?"

The boy glanced at his ragged clothes and his bare toes showing through the sides of his heavy boots; and he thought of the

1 John 1:12.

miserable hole under the steps of the cellar, which he called his home; and he shook his head with a very positive shake.

"But you may, Tom," continued Mr. Hope, laying his hand upon the lad's shoulder; "as sure as you are hearkening to me this minute, so sure the Lord Jesus is now ready to give you the right to become one of God's sons, and His own brother, for He is not ashamed to call us brothers. You have only to trust in Him, just the same as you are trusting and believing in me. If you become the son of God, and the brother of the Lord Jesus Christ, there'd be no more stealing or lying then, my boy, and no more fear of the police; only good, honest, hard work, and God's blessing upon it; and by-and-bye warm clothes, and good food, and a better home to live in; and at the last, when you die, a happy home for ever in heaven. Tom, should you like it?"

Tom stood silent for a minute or two with his eyes cast down and his hands clenched, pondering over the strange things his new friend had been saying to him. He had but a vague idea of their meaning yet, but there was a bright comfort in the thought of another father than the one who was in jail. After a while he lifted up his eyes, dim with tears, which could not altogether hide the anxiety dwelling in them.

"I hope it's true," he said; "and please, sir, I should like it very much; but I don't seem to know nothing about it."

"Now, then, this is what you shall do for me," said Mr. Hope; "instead of you paying me any money for getting you off this time, you shall do your best to learn to read before I come again. You are a sharp lad, I know; and if you set your mind upon it, you'll know how to read a little before I am in Manchester again. I've spoken to Banner, and he promises me he will find a night-school where they will teach you well. Will you do this for me, Tom?"

"Ay, will I!" said the boy.

"And little Phil as well," said Mr. Hope, smiling. "Banner will tell you when I am coming again, and I shall expect to see you quite a different fellow. How do you mean to get your living, Tom?"

"I'll try not to steal," answered Tom, earnestly; "indeed I never took to it much, sir. I'll go out with Phil, selling chips or salt; there's many folks'll buy from Phil when they won't from me."

"Tom," said Mr. Hope, "I'll trust you with some money to start upon. Look me right in the face, and promise me you'll not spend it in drink, or lose it at pitch-and-toss, or waste it in any way, but you'll try to make an honest living by it."

"I will, sir," said Tom, with a sob.

Mr. Hope put a golden sovereign into his hand, and Tom gazed at it in speechless amazement. Such a sum of money had never been in his possession, scarcely in his thoughts, before. He tried to mutter some thanks, but Mr. Hope told him it was time for him to go now, and he made his way with a heavy and shambling tread down the long room, feeling rich beyond the most extravagant dreams that could have entered into his head. He had no pocket he could trust the precious coin to, and his hand was not safe enough, but before opening the door he stowed it carefully into his mouth, between his cheek and his teeth. Banner had only time enough to lead him to the entrance-hall, where Alice and Phil were waiting for him, and to dismiss them with a friendly glance. Tom tread quietly down the great staircase into the busy street, already subdued by his wealth, and the cares enkindled[1] by it, while Alice on one side, and Phil on the other, were both telling eagerly of the good fortune that had befallen Phil in the shape of the lady's sixpence.

---

1 Enkindled—aroused into action.

Chapter 5

THE FEAST IN PILGRIM STREET

om was very sparing of speech as they walked along the street, for the sovereign in his mouth made it difficult to talk; but Alice, who knew nothing about it, was disappointed at his silence, and soon left off speaking herself. Presently they reached the corner of the street leading to Tom's old home, and here he came to a dead stop. He had heard Handforth's wife screaming and crying loudly in the court, when the judge sentenced her husband to seven years' imprisonment, and he scarcely knew whether it would be safe to show himself at her house. Alice saw the doubt and hesitation which troubled him, and she spoke heartily and eagerly.

"You're to come on home with me," she said; "you and Phil; father said so. Phil and me are going to buy something for tea with the lady's sixpence. You go on, Tom, and tell the little ones we're coming. We won't be long after you."

Tom was not sorry to be alone for a little while, but he did not hurry on to Pilgrim Street. He turned up a quiet road by the cathedral, and crouching down under the palisades round the cathedral yard, he took the glittering coin out of his mouth and rubbed it dry upon the sleeve of his jacket, while he kept a jealous and wary look-out lest anybody should come within sight of it. It was very bright and beautiful. He held it deep in the hollow of his hand, and let the sun shine upon it. His fingers tingled at the touch of it. He had a vague recollection of the words Mr. Hope had spoken to him, but they awoke very faint emotions compared to the delight of feeling and handling this real piece of gold. Play at pitch-and-toss with it! He caught his breath at the very thought of such a thing, for he could not even venture to hold it lightly in his fingers, and it lay in one palm covered with the other, while he only indulged himself with frequent glimpses at it. How could he ever bring himself to change it? And yet it would have to come to that, he supposed. He almost wished he had not let Alice and Phil go away to waste the six-pence; he might have started with that, and it would have lasted over a day; but he felt a little pinch of shame at the thought, and rousing himself from his solitary pleasure, he replaced the sover-eign in his mouth, and ran off towards Pilgrim Street.

When Tom opened the door, after a loud single knock at it, for he had never before been there as a friend and visitor, he found that Alice and Phil had reached home before him. Half of Phil's sixpence had bought half-a-dozen herrings, for it was a plentiful herring season, and as it was getting near the eve-ning, Alice had been able to get them for a halfpenny apiece. The other threepence had been spent in tea, Alice saying there was plenty of bread at home. When Tom made his appearance, Phil and the four little Pendleburys were hovering with delight round the plate of beautiful fish, longing for tea-time to arrive. Tea was not to be thought of before six o'clock, when the father would come in, and the mill be "loosed" where Kitty Pendle-bury was at work; but until then there was the pleasure of look-ing at the silvery scales of the fish glistening in the scanty light which visited the cellar. In spite of the general joy Tom was quite still, and sat by the handful of fire as if he were cold, though it was a warm day in August, and Alice only kindled the fire to boil the kettle and fry the herrings. Tom began to feel embarrassed with his riches, for there were many things he would have said to Alice and Phil but for the difficulty he felt in speaking freely.

"Tom," said Alice, almost in a whisper, while the little ones were busy near the door, "Tom, aren't you glad to be set free? Father and me were so glad, we couldn't tell you;" and Tom saw her wipe her eyes with her apron as she stooped down over the fire.

"Miss Alice," he said in a thick voice, "I don't mind telling you; you're safe, anyhow. Look here!" and he gave her a sudden vision of the sovereign flashing for an instant in the light of the blazing chips.

"Oh, Tom," she cried, "how ever did you came by it? Oh, Tom!"

"It's all right," said Tom; "that gentleman, he gave it me; him who got me off. It's to begin life with, and I'm to make my fortune—mine and little Phil's. Did you ever have as much?"

"No," answered Alice; "but father had one once."

The sovereign made Alice quite as serious as Tom, and she sat in sober thought until the cathedral clock struck six, and the children crowded round her and the fire to watch the hissing and spluttering of the fish in the frying-pan, while each one held a plate to warm by the brief heat of the chips. The tea had been made some time ago in a tin teapot, which was kept warm on the hob, and the tea and the fish filled Nat Pendlebury's cellar with a pleasant fragrance. It was, without doubt, a noble feast to celebrate Tom's escape from imprisonment, and now he had shared his secret with Alice, he was sufficiently at ease to take some interest in the meal. By some means or other the children knew at once when their father had turned into Pilgrim Street, and they ran to meet him, and to bring him in with a tumult of gladness.

"Bless thee, Tom!" cried Nat, stretching out both his hands to him; "welcome out of jail a hundred times. I wish I'd only known thee was there before, and a word or two from me and Alice could get thee out. But it's done thee no harm, my lad, I'll be bound. Alice, my lass, we'll treat ourselves to a tablecloth this night. There now! I'll lay it all right and straight. Kitty's mill is loosed, and she'll be here to the minute. Now then, children, for the table-cloth and the crocks."

Nat was not still for a moment while he was speaking. He prepared the table-cloth by selecting and unfolding two large posting-bills, one blue and one red, and spread them neatly on the table, with the printed side downwards, upon which he laid all the knives and forks which the house contained, and the plates that had been warming at the fire. Before all his arrangements were completed Kitty came, and every one was listening and looking at the last hiss of taking the last herring from the pan, which Alice accomplished with great dexterity and composure.

"Just like her poor mother!" said Nat to himself. "Why, my dears," he added, rubbing his wiry hair with sudden excitement, "which of us can remember the chapter Alice read out of the Testament last night, all about that great multitude of people whom the Lord Jesus fed with bread and fishes? Just the same as us, Joey, wasn't it? And they sat down on the grass, didn't they, Suey? Well, we can't sit on the grass, but Phil and the three smallest shall have the little bench, and Suey must come on my knee, and Tom, you bring up that old box to the table, and Alice have mother's rocking-chair, and Kitty sit on the stool. There! now we're all ready and comfortable."

They were all more than ready, devouring with their eyes

the plate of fish which Alice had placed before her father. The largest was picked out to be divided between Alice and Kitty, who declared, both of them, that they could not possibly eat a whole herring at once; the next largest was allotted to Tom, because he had so narrowly escaped being sent to jail; and the third, everybody said, must be for father. After that, the very smallest was given to Phil, who had a whole one to himself, as being both a guest and the giver of the feast; and the remaining two were divided among the four little ones. Never had finer or better flavored herrings been caught in the Irish Sea, and they took a very long time to be eaten, especially by Alice, who was kept busy with the tin teapot and the brown mugs. But the feast came to an end at last, like all other feasts, and the children had their hands and faces wiped by Alice; and as soon as the tea-things had been cleared away, they took their seats again quietly and Alice brought out of a drawer a small Bible, which Tom at once knew was the strange book he had seen before.

"Now, little ones," said Nat, looking round him with a beaming smile, and hugging Suey in his arms, "as it's a feast night, and Tom hasn't been sent to jail, you shall choose the place for Alice to read. Is there anything Tom 'ud choose, particular?"

"I don't know," answered Tom; "it's all fresh to me."

"Let's have little Samuel," whispered Suey in her father's ear.

"Suey chooses little Samuel," said Nat; "who else speaks for him?"

There was a division of opinion for two or three minutes, but at length it was decided that little Samuel was the best choice that could be made. Alice read about the Lord calling the child while he was asleep, and Phil listened with all his heart set upon it; but Tom's thoughts were divided between the new story and the sovereign, which had been the only hindrance to his complete enjoyment of the feast. When the chapter was ended they all knelt down, and Nat prayed in a voice which was a little tremulous,[1] as if he were going to cry.

"O Lord," he said, "please to call every one of these children, like little Samuel; and me and Tom too, and all of us. Lord, make us very thankful for the bread and fishes Thou hast fed us with; like the great multitude when they sat down on the green grass. O Lord, make Tom very thankful he isn't in jail tonight. Take care of Kitty when she's at work in the mill; and bless Alice, and all the little ones, 'specially Phil. Joey wants some new clogs, Lord, and so does Phil; they're both barefoot, and I'd be very thankful if Thee will think about it, and send them some; only, to be sure, Thou know what is best, Lord. We pray Thee to forgive us all our sins, and keep us safe all night; for the sake of Thy Son Jesus Christ, who died to save us. Amen."

Then Nat and the children repeated "Our Father," slowly and solemnly; and Tom could hear the voice of Phil join in whenever he could remember a word or two. As soon as prayers were over Alice and the four youngest children and Phil withdrew behind a partition which screened off one end of the cellar, and which was covered with posters of many colors. Those who were left, Nat, Kitty, and Tom, drew their seats nearer to the open door, for the evening was warm, and the only air that entered the cellar came from the close little street above. They were very quiet, for Kitty was half asleep, and Tom was pondering in his own mind whether he could trust Nat enough to ask his advice about the sovereign, when a shadow fell upon them from the pavement above, and looking up, they saw Banner preparing to descend the steps to Nat's door.

---

1 Tremulous—trembling or shaking.

Chapter 6

THE POLICEMAN'S GOSPEL

anner cast a keen policeman's eye round the cellar, and took note in his own mind of the supper of fried fish, the scent of which still lingered in the close dwelling. He nodded stiffly to Alice, as she came round the screen, and reached forward her rocking-chair for him to sit upon. It was the safest and strongest chair in the house, but Banner did not feel at ease upon it as he sat bolt upright, after pushing it far back into the shade, lest any passer-by should catch a glimpse of the strange sight of a policeman seemingly upon friendly and familiar terms with the occupants of a cellar. After Nat had bade him welcome, an uncomfortable silence fell upon them all, which disquieted Tom greatly, until Banner broke it by addressing him in a measured and authoritative tone.

"Thomas Haslam," he said, "you've escaped justice this time, and I've made a promise to Mr. Hope that I'll keep my eye upon you till he comes again. You'll not find it easy to get from under my eye, but if you do, there's another Eye upon you, which never sleeps night nor day, and which you can't hide yourself from, even if you hide yourself from me. That Eye sees into your very thoughts. It is the Eye of God, who is present everywhere. He knows all you say and do. He can tell what you mean to do tomorrow, and He keeps a strict account of it all. There's a dreadful book, Thomas, in which the whole of your life is written. Did you ever tell a lie?—every lie you've ever told is put down in it. Did you ever steal?—it is all put down in it. There's a verse of a hymn you'd better learn. I'll say it for you—

'There's not a sin that we commit,
        Nor wicked word we say,
But in His dreadful book 'tis writ,
        Against the judgment day!'

—Ah! Thomas, at the last judgment-day, when all the angels and men and devils are before the throne of God, that book will be read out, and they will listen to every wicked thing you ever did, or spoke, or thought of. What do you think of that, Thomas Haslam?"

It was growing dusk in the dark cellar, and the faces which Tom had seen smiling about him began to look pale and gloomy in the shade. Nat was shaking his head thoughtfully, and Alice's eyes were cast down; while of Banner little could be seen except the outline of his stern face, and the glistening of his keen eyes. Tom felt a thousand untold fears awakening him; and the sovereign, which he had been holding fondly but stealthily in the palm of his hand, lay very heavily upon it. He did not quite know whether Banner could see it; but it was quite certain that God did.

"Mr. Banner," he said hesitatingly, "I've got a sovereign Mr. Hope gave to me to set up business with. Please, what shall I do with it?"

The sovereign quite changed the current of Banner's thoughts, and very quickly he and Nat were discussing with eager interest the very best way of laying it out to advantage.

For some time past Tom and Phil had been selling chips and salt up the Longsight road, and had established a sort of connection there, which had been broken off by Tom's unmerited imprisonment. But Tom was ambitious; with so much money in hand it would be possible to take a bold step on in life—no doubt the feast of the evening had something to do with it—when Alice suggested the sale of herrings.

"I'd been thinking of it," cried Nat, in a glow of enthusiasm; "and now Alice has hit on it too, I'd say by all manner of means, do it, Tom. I know an old man that owns a donkey and a donkey-cart, but he's laid up just now with rheumatism, and it was only the other day he asked me, did I know any decent chap as wanted to hire a donkey-cart. Now, if Tom could take a good lot of things, say chips at the bottom, and herrings at the top, he could sell the herrings as he went out in time for folks' dinners, and the chips coming back, ready to light the fire next morning, and so make a rare good thing of it. But old Crocker is mighty particular about his donkey. Could you promise to use it fair, Tom?"

"Ay," answered Tom, "I'd never hurt a poor dumb creature."

It was some time before the subject could be fully settled; but at last Banner decided that it might be tried, and that Nat and Tom should see the owner of the donkey-cart the next day. It was getting late now, and Nat grew visibly uneasy, until at last he invited Banner to accompany him behind the screen, where the children lay sleeping soundly.

"Sir," he said, "Tom 'ud be heartily welcome, but I've no accommodation for him for the night. That's Alice's, and Kitty's, and Suey's bed; and this holds the three little ones, only Phil makes four, and they are lying crosswise. I get a shake-down before the fire, which is very warm of a winter's night, and not so hard as you'd think. I wish I could keep Tom for the night; but perhaps you'd see after him?"

"Certainly," answered Banner. "Come, Thomas Haslam, it's time for you and me to march. I'll take care of your sovereign till tomorrow."

Tom felt a pang of dread and grief when he saw Banner drop the precious coin carelessly into his pocket, but he did not dream of objecting; and presently he was walking resignedly in the policeman's steps through the dusky streets, in the direction of his old lodgings, where he told Banner he had left a few small possessions. When they reached the abode of Will Handforth's family, they found it already deserted, and every article of the scanty furniture removed; but the key was left in the lock outside the door. In the old hole under the steps the straw still remained, and there Tom could pass the night as usual. Banner stood straight and erect in the middle of the empty cellar, feeling that he must not leave Tom until he had deepened the impression his words had made upon him. How much misery might have been saved to both of them had Banner known, and Tom heard, of the love of God as well as His justice!

"Thomas," he said, "I fear you know nothing about God. He is Almighty, and can do whatever He will. He does everything in heaven and earth according to His own pleasure. He could crush you to death as easily as I crush this moth," and Banner caught one of the evening moths which were fluttering round his lamp, and held out his large finger and thumb that the boy might see the fine atoms of grey dust which was all that remained of the busy insect; "that's how He could kill you. Once He struck a man and woman dead in a moment for telling a lie, and He can do the same to you. He cannot endure sin, and He will slay every sinner by the breath of His mouth. You know yourself to be a sinner, Thomas?"

"Ay," murmured Tom, with a shiver of fright; "I've been a bad boy."

"That's true," continued Banner; "and you don't know the half, or the hundredth part of your sins as God knows them. He has kept counting them up ever since you were born, and not one of them can be forgotten or left out of His reckoning. Thomas, it was a dreadful thing to face the judge, and see his eye upon you, when you stood at the bar, wasn't it?"

"Ay," answered Tom.

"Yet that judge did not know whether you were guilty or innocent," said Banner; "and the jury had to try you. But God Almighty will not want a jury to help Him. And that judge could do no more than send you to jail for a few years at most; but God Almighty is able to cast both your soul and body into hell. Oh, there'll be a grand assize at the last day! The trumpets will sound, and the dead will rise out of their graves, and the Judge will sit upon His awful throne, and the books will be opened. Then every man will be judged according to what is written in the books. What is written in your book, Thomas Haslam? Lying, and swearing, and thieving, and Sabbath-breaking, and every sin you have been guilty of, ever since you were born. It's a thousand times worse to stand before that Judge than before the judge you saw this morning."

Banner paused; and Tom ventured to remove his eyes from his stern face, and glance round the deserted and miserable dwelling, so empty and secret-looking, but still all open to the eye of the dreadful God of whom Banner had been speaking. He wished within himself that the policeman would stay a long time; but he did not know how to detain him, and already he was moving as if about to depart, and to take the friendly light away with him. He only stayed to read the story of Ananias and Sapphira, of whom Tom had never heard before, and then he prepared to go.

"Good night, Thomas," he said; "I hope you will remember

what I've said, and begin from this night to grow up a God-fearing man."

The last thing that Tom saw was the flaming eye of the policeman's lamp turned full upon him as Banner closed the door. He crawled into his hole, and lay down upon the straw; but he could not sleep. For the last three weeks he had enjoyed the luxury of a clean bed, in a cell which he had shared with Handforth and his thoughts went back regretfully to the jail. As he tossed to and fro, the words of Banner came back again and again to his mind: "God Almighty can crush you as I crush this moth." Who could tell but that He might do it that very night, while he lay alone in the horrible solitude? He had a vague idea that death would not be the last of him, but something more terrible was to follow. God had been counting up his sins, and putting them into a book, ever since he was born; and He was going to judge him for them. Tom knew what a judge was. Well, he would leave off his sins as fast as he could, and he would learn to read and write, if that would pacify God. He only wished he could get somewhere out of God's sight for a little while, until he could make himself more fit to meet His awful eye. But Banner said He could always see him; and He could not only see the outside of him, which men could see, but He could look into his very heart, and search out all the wickedness which was hidden there. He knew what he was thinking of at that moment. How could he sleep if God's eye was looking at him through the black darkness? Maybe He would speak too, as He spoke to Samuel when he was asleep. How fearful it would be to hear God's voice in the dead silence! Tom started up in a fever of affright, and stared into the blackness about him, till a myriad of little specks of brightness, which gave no light, seemed to dance before his eyes; and his straining ear caught the distant rolling of wheels along the street which passed the end of the alley. With a muttered oath, and a quicker throbbing of the heart when he thought that he had been swearing again, he sank back upon his straw bed; and before he was aware of it, he fell into an uneasy slumber, which was haunted by horrid dreams.

Chapter 7

BRIGHT PROSPECTS

At a convenient time the next day Nat accompanied Tom to the house of old Crocker, the owner of the donkey and donkey-cart, with whom they made a very good bargain. The old man was pleased with the manner in which Tom handled the donkey's ear, and scratched his long nose; and the donkey himself seemed to accept him willingly as his master. Crocker said he would sooner let Tom have him for a shilling a-day, than most boys for eighteen pence. It was agreed that he should pay that sum each day in advance, and keep the donkey in food. When the bargain was struck, Tom was obliged to change his beautiful sovereign, which he did with a thrill of regret; but there was no help for it. He forgot his regret the next morning, however, when at five o'clock he and Phil, with Nat as a friend and adviser, drove to Shude Hill market to stock his donkey-cart.

It was not a very handsome cart; in truth it was little more than a few rough boards, hanging loosely together upon an old axle-tree and wheels. But both Tom and Phil were intensely proud of it, and after they had purchased some herrings and potatoes, for, as Nat observed, folks could not eat herrings without potatoes or bread, and after they had driven to a wood-yard,

TOM'S START IN LIFE.

and closed a hard bargain for a stock of chips, they started back again triumphantly, in the early sunshine, to Pilgrim Street. From Pilgrim Street, though it was something out of their way, they were to set off on their first day's round, and Alice was to make the very first purchase from Tom; for it was a known fact amongst all the neighbors that Alice's handsel[1] was lucky; and if the dwellers in Pilgrim Street could only persuade her to lay out a penny with them before they started out with their goods, they were sure to be lucky all day. Alice, and all the rest, including Kitty, for it was not yet six o'clock, and the mill did not open till then, were watching for their appearance at the bottom of the street; and every one gathered about the donkey-cart, while Alice made her selection of the chips and potatoes she required.

At last they fairly started off, Nat with Suey in his arms waving his old cap, and all the lot cheering after them as long as they were in sight. Then Tom saw that business was about to begin, and he was gravely happy as he trudged up Market Street at the donkey's head, while little Phil sat proudly in front of the cart. They passed Banner on the way, and he gave them as benignant[2] a smile and nod as could be expected from a policeman in a stiff stock; and Tom wished that Will Handforth, and others of his old comrades, could have seen it. But a wide gulf seemed to lie between himself and these old companions already. He had taken a great stride towards decent respectability and honesty, and he trembled at the thought of falling back. If he met any of his former friends he would show them pretty plainly he meant to have nothing to do with them.

"Tom," said Phil, leaning forward, and touching him with a green branch given to him by a market-woman, "Tom, last night I dreamt God called me, like little Samuel."

---

1 Hansel—The first act of using any thing; the first sale.
2 Benignant—kind, gracious or favorable.

Tom had had no dream like that, as he fell asleep in his solitary hole—for the cellar still remained unoccupied by any regular tenant—but his thoughts had been again of the dreadful God who never ceased to watch him for a single moment. But now, as he looked back at Phil, he was amazed to see how bright his face was, and what a light shone in his blue eyes. It was a clear, fair face now, for Alice took care to wash it well, and Phil looked very beautiful in Tom's eyes.

"Why, Phil, old fellow," said Tom, "that was nice, wasn't it?"

"Ay!" cried Phil, with a glad smile; "and I dreamt I tried to look up into God's face, but I couldn't, it was so bright, like the sun. Just try to look at the sun, Tom, and see how thy eyes'll wink."

The sun was shining the more brightly because the smoke from the factories had not yet clouded the atmosphere, and though Tom's eyes were strong, the lids closed as the light poured down upon them.

"That's not nice," he said; "it dazes me."

"And I was dazed," continued Phil; "and I thought God told me I should see His face some day, if I waited, and was a good boy. He said He'd make my eyes strong enough; and I thought I was going to ask Him to let thee see His face, Tom, and then I woke up."

Tom walked on silently, for they were getting near to Ardwick and Longsight, and it was time to give himself wholly to business. The servants were beginning to light their fires, and he sold a few bundles of chips, and some of the herrings to be cooked for breakfast. As the morning wore on, he and little Phil marched slowly through the streets, crying in their shrillest tones, "Herring! fresh herring! fine herring!" until they grew quite brave. But they were very fortunate in selling them, so much so that Tom treated himself and Phil to a small meat pie, hot from the oven, about noon; and they ate it leisurely under the side-arch of a railway bridge, while the donkey feasted upon a few handsful of hay and a turnip. Before six in the evening they had disposed of all their stock, and they wended their way slowly back again to Pilgrim Street, weary, but happy, the bag which Alice had made for their money being heavy with copper coins.

There was something mysterious about the manner of Nat and Alice as they greeted their return, but Tom was too much elated, and too much engrossed in his own affairs, to perceive it. He emptied the money-bag carefully upon the table, and kneeling down beside it, he counted the pence into little heaps, each worth a shilling. It took both him and Nat a long time to do it, while Alice and Phil looked on eagerly, anxious to hear what was the result of the day's work. At last it was discovered that after every expense was paid, including the meat-pie, there remained a clear profit of one shilling and one penny, which Nat put on one side by themselves with an air of delight.

"It'll be two shillings tomorrow, Tom," he said; "mark my words, thee'lt have two shillings clear tomorrow. Not such a poor do, is it, my lad? Thee'lt make thy fortune some day, Tom. And now we've some good news to tell, haven't we, Alice? Something about thee, and Phil, and Polly, and all of us."

Tom's heart beat quickly. For a moment it flashed across his mind that perhaps his father had been released from prison with a ticket-of-leave, and his heart sank within him, and his brown face paled. But surely Nat would not look so joyful about that, nor would Alice fold her hands together, and purse up her lips as if she could hardly keep from speaking it all out at once, and smile with such a beaming face.

"Thee couldn't give a guess, I suppose?" asked Nat.

"No," said Tom, faintly.

"It'll be the real making of little Phil," Nat went on, laying his hand fondly on the child's curly head; "there'll be no more clemming for him, poor little lad, but good clothes and good victuals, and a good bed, and good learning. They'll make a scholar of him, Tom, and Alice says he'll make a gradely good one. 'Bless the Lord, O my soul, and forget not all His benefits.' We'll read that psalm tonight, Alice."

"Yes, father," said Alice.

"Not but what we might read it every night of our lives," continued Nat, thoughtfully; "but it 'ud maybe get all the same to us. Tom, thee minds the night we had the tea-drinking, how I told the Lord that Joey and Phil wanted some new clogs? I knew He could send them, and would, somehow or other, by giving me an extra job or two, or somehow. And here they are, Tom. Joey's got his on, and ran out with the little ones to show the neighbors, and Alice has got Phil's. Where are they, my love?"

They were in her pocket, which was constructed to carry many things that were safer out of the little ones' reach; and she speedily drew them out, a good pair of strong clogs, new from the maker's, such as had never been on Phil's feet before.

"That's not all," said Nat, laying his hand impressively upon Tom's shoulder; "and now I'll tell thee all about it. I was gone out with my bills, and Alice was all alone here with the children, when Joey runs in to say Mr. Banner was at the end of the street, with a lady in a grand carriage—a grand carriage, Alice?"

"Yes, father," said Alice; "very grand, with two horses."

"Two horses," repeated Nat; "very good. So the lady gets out of the grand carriage, Tom, and Mr. Banner he walks before her straight up to our house. Alice, the house was clean and tidy, I hope, my dear?"

"Pretty well, father," answered Alice.

"Just so," continued Nat; "so she came in, and sat down on Alice's rocking-chair ——"

"In a blue silk dress and silk mantle," interrupted Alice; "and a white bonnet, with a blue feather in it."

"Exactly," resumed Nat; "I can see her as plain as in a picture. And says she, 'I'm Mr. Hope's sister.' And who is her husband, dost thou think? Kitty's master! Ay, Kitty's mill is his. And who should she be but the very lady that gave Phil the sixpence! And she sends her footman, Tom—wasn't it her footman, Alice?—to buy these clogs for Joey and Phil. And she promised to pay for Polly's schooling and Joey's."

Nat came to a full pause, and looked steadily into Tom's astonished face, and then burst into a long and happy laugh, which no one could resist, until all of them laughed together; little Phil the loudest and longest, as he drew the clogs on to his hands, Alice saying that his feet would want washing before he tried on his new possessions.

"But that isn't all," cried Nat, when the laughter had subsided; "bless you, Tom, that's not half of Phil's fortune. Why, thee knows a fine big house on Ardwick Green, side by side with the gentlefolk's houses, where there's a school for boys and girls? They take them in and feed them, and lodge them, and learn them all sorts of things, and put them out into a way of getting their own living when they've done with them. Well, listen, Tom! She is going to get them to take little Phil. There's for thee!"

Nat gave Tom a slight push, and fell back a step or two, ready for another burst of laughter. But for some reason or other it did not come. Tom's eyes and mouth were wide open, but more with surprise than delight. If little Phil were separated from him, he would feel very lonely indeed; especially now that there was such a gulf between him and his old comrades. He had been reckoning upon always having him to ride in his donkey-cart, and sit under railway arches to share his dinner. But he could not help seeing what a capital thing it would be for his bright little Phil. As Nat said, there would be no more starving, no more shivering in wintry weather, no fluttering rags and naked feet; but a good comfortable home, and good teaching secured to him, and no risk about whether the donkey-cart was lucky or not. Yes; it would be a good thing for Phil, doubtless; but Tom's heart felt heavy at the prospect of parting with him, until he remembered how much more money he could earn if the cost of Phil's living was taken off his shoulders. That thought cheered his spirits a little; and although he did not encourage Nat in a hearty laugh as before, his face relaxed into a smile, and he said it was a rare good fortune for little Phil.

Chapter 8

TOM IN BUSINESS

Though it was rare good fortune, it was a sad day both for Tom and Phil too when he entered the school on Ardwick Green. But everybody said it would make a man of Phil; and Alice, as she kissed him tenderly with tears in her eyes, told him she was sure he would make a grand scholar some day or other, and perhaps grow too grand for them all. Besides all this, the master of the school promised to let him have a holiday pretty often, if he was a good boy, and said that Tom might come to see him occasionally. So Phil passed away out of Tom's sight within the doors of the school, and there was to be no more starving or rags for him.

Then Tom, having nothing else to care for, gave himself up to business, like many a thousand more of the people dwelling in the great city, who never thought of the God who cared for them. The cellar had been let to a decent man and his wife who had no family, and were glad to let Tom keep his own hole in it, and who were far quieter and tidier than the Handforths had ever been. So Tom was no longer alone at night, and his dreadful dreams no longer troubled him. The last thing at night, and the first thing in the morning, his thought was, how he could get enough money to have once more a real shining sovereign lying in the hollow of his hand. His object was not easy to gain, for both Banner and Nat urged him to lay out his money in buying more decent clothes; his trade would profit by it, they said, and Tom proved their words to be true, though he felt it to be a great trouble thus to part with his hardly-earned savings. Banner took him more openly under his patronage as he began to present a more respectable appearance, and he spoke to some of the servants in his beat in his behalf, and recommended him as a boy worthy of trust and encouragement. So Tom met with plenty of customers, and had many an errand confided to him by which he earned a few additional pence. In the course of a few months he found himself well fitted out with suitable clothes, and to his great joy, after collecting almost stealthily penny after penny, and changing them into silver, and carrying them always about him in Alice's money-bag, he was at last able to obtain the sovereign he had so long coveted.

Banner also took care to get Tom into a night-school belonging to Mr. Watson's parish, where he himself had a class, having at the commencement of it been engaged to be there in his office of policeman. It was natural that he should wish to have Tom under his own eye, for he was beginning to feel a friendly interest in him; and though the boy did not know it, he was anxious to be a true friend to him, as he had promised Mr. Hope. He wished to instruct him in religion, and to give him such a knowledge of God, and of His laws, as would deter him from falling back into his old ways. So Banner laboured hard with Tom and the class of rough lads, teaching them the commandments and the awful penalties of breaking them, with the most terrible of the threatenings which he found scattered up and down in his Bible. Whenever Banner came upon any text which made him think of God as an all-seeing and all-searching Judge, he treasured it up to repeat, with explanations of his own, to

his class at the night-school. He was very much in earnest, and
every now and then he succeeded in gaining the awe-stricken
attention of the boys, as he drew fearful pictures of the conse-
quences of sin; and Tom especially would fasten his bright black
eyes upon him and drink in every word, and tremble, and grow
pale with terror. It was no wonder that Banner considered him
changed and converted. He was tidy, and industrious, and careful, and very eager to learn to read and write, and Banner began
to take pleasure in the thought that Tom was a brand which he
had plucked from the burning.

But the true effect of Banner's teaching was to make the
boy's heart at first miserable, and then hard. For a while he tried
to do right in order to pacify his angry God and Judge, but
his conscience, once awakened to the knowledge of God's commandments, could not be satisfied without a perfect obedience
to them. Often, from the force of long habit, he fell into the
utterance of oaths, and in an instant the third commandment
rose up in accusation against him. He knew himself to be a
Sabbath-breaker, a liar, and a thief, and he never could consent
to love and honor his wicked father. All these old sins hung still
about him as heavy fetters, and Banner, with all his earnestness,
did not make it clear to him how, through the love of Christ, he
could be set free. So, after two or three fruitless struggles, he at
last grew hardened to his sins. If God did all things in heaven
and earth to please Himself, as Banner taught him, then it was
He who had put him into this position, and given to him such a
wicked father. His laws were too difficult to keep, so he must go
on to the end, and stand before the Judge at the last day, to be
driven for ever from His presence with the devil and his angels.

Poor Tom! He was very wretched, but he did not know how
to make his wretchedness known to any one who could help
him. He had nothing to turn to for comfort, now that Phil was

parted from him, except his money, for Banner kept so strict a watch upon him that he could scarcely sink back to his former degraded habits. Once he lingered under the bright windows of a gin-palace, where a girl was playing on a tambourine, and he felt a strong inclination to turn in; but at that moment he saw the shining hat and large buttons of a policeman coming up the street, and he fled swiftly. Every policeman brought Banner to his mind, and kept him in wholesome fear of being caught in doing wrong; and as one or another might be seen at every turn, he was delivered from much evil. That is, of evil from without; within, there was a canker[1] eating away his heart, and bringing him into as bitter a bondage as any which had made him a slave before.

Tom had two sources of great dread. First he dreaded the release of his father from prison, and his return to any kind of authority over himself. He hated and feared him with intense bitterness; and he would have counted the day of his death as a day of rejoicing and gladness. But he was not dead. From time to time there came to him, by some mysterious means, a message from the distant jail where his father was working out his long sentence, that he should soon be free on a ticket-of-leave, and that he would come back to Phil and him in Manchester. One of these messages had reached him since his own trial with Handforth for house-breaking; and for a day or two Tom had been strongly tempted to give up the effort to be steady, and industrious, and honest. Every day his dread and hatred of his father grew more profound.

But the other dread was, after all, a keener and deeper misery. The terrors of God were upon him. Once he could sin confidently and comfortably; but now his inmost spirit trembled and shrank at the remembrance that God saw him always. He

1 Canker—anything that corrupts or destroys.

was afraid of many things which had never alarmed him before. In the summer storms, when the thunder rolled louder than the roar of the streets, and the lightning flashed amongst the thick clouds, he fancied that God was about to strike him dead for his sins. But when winter came, and it was pitch dark in the morning, and the night came on early, he suspected every footstep behind him was that of a thief who would snatch from him his hardly-earned savings. From this latter fear he freed himself by intrusting the secret of his cherished wealth to Banner, by whose advice he put it in the Post-Office Savings Bank. But he himself was not safe; nor could he hide himself from God. God was searching out and reckoning up all his sins; and sooner or later He would summon him to give an account of all that he had done.

There was a short season of relief and brightness at the next spring assizes, when Banner took him to the house of Mrs. Worthington, Mr. Hope's sister, with whom Mr. Hope was staying. Banner spoke cordially of his conduct since his friend had given him a start in life, and Tom felt a glow of joy and pride as he heard the rare sound of his own praises. Mr. Hope was glad to hear them also, and he shook hands with him as a friend, and gave him a Bible, in which he found out one special verse, and told Tom to try to read it. Tom had still to spell the longer words, but he made out this sentence, "He that overcometh shall inherit all things; and I will be his God, and he shall be my son."[1] He did not understand it, but as he spelt it through with difficulty, the words were impressed upon his mind: as yet only like the seed which lies as if it were dead and decayed, but in reality quickening into life under the surface of the soil.

---

1 Revelation 21:7.

Chapter 9

TEMPTATION, FALL AND FLIGHT

ore than twelve months had passed away since Tom had made his first start in trade; and now every morning at sunrise his donkey-cart might be seen well laden with fruit, fish, or vegetables, purchased in Shude Hill market at wholesale prices. He was in a fair way of establishing a very good business in the round which he had chosen, and he had already some thought of exchanging his rough and shaky truck for a smart little cart, painted blue, with red spokes to the wheels, upon which should be conspicuously painted, "Thomas Haslam, Fruiterer and Greengrocer." Banner smiled graciously upon this plan, for Tom had seven pounds in the Savings' Bank, and was putting by three or four shillings every week regularly. A very precious book to Tom was his Savings Bank book; and as his love of money struck deeper and deeper root, it became a far more delightful study than the Bible which Mr. Hope had given to him.

It happened one day that he had finished his round earlier than usual, and was in time to take his book to the Post-Office before the hour of closing. He had five shillings to deposit, a larger sum than he had ever before saved in a week, and his eyes sparkled with gratification as he put down the book upon the counter, with two half-crowns upon it. The clerk took up the money, looked at one of the pieces suspiciously, and then returned it to Tom. Yes, it was without question a bad one, and Tom's heart sank like lead. How could he who was so keen and sharp have taken a bad half-crown? But the clerk was about to seize and forfeit it, and the loss would be completely his.

"Please, sir," cried Tom, readily, but with great anxiety, "I know where I took the half-crown, in a shop up Downing Street; and they'll be sure to remember it, and change it for me, if I take it back."

"Very well, my lad," said the clerk, who knew Tom well by sight, and regarded him with favor because he was always civil in his manner; "you may take the half-crown then."

Tom made haste out of the office, with the bad money in his hand, and ran swiftly out of sight, lest the clerk should change his mind, and insist upon having it back again. He could not think how he could have been so cheated, or where he could have taken it; for it was a ready-made lie, which he had spoken so glibly to the clerk. He sauntered away homewards, with his head cast down, and his eyes fastened upon the ground, in deep thought; but he could in no way recall how it had passed into his possession. At any rate, thought he, it would never pay for him to be at the loss of it. Whoever had given it to him had received the full worth of his money; and why should he, a poor boy, without friends or helpers of any kind, lose so large a sum out of his earnings? He owed a few shillings to a greengrocer, who had a standing in Shude Hill market, and he would go this evening and pay him the debt.

Tom waited until it was quite dusk, before he started off for Shude Hill market. It was a busy time, for the women and girls, who had been at work in the mills all day, were thronging to the market to buy something they could relish for their supper. The

gas-lights were flaring and flickering in the evening breeze over
the stalls of crockery, and second-hand clothing, and drapery,
and fruit, and fish; and there was scarcely room to get along the
narrow walks, through the crowd of people who were gathered
round the standings. Here and there the stall-keepers were getting their tea, and sitting round braziers, in which smouldered
a few red cinders; for the evenings were growing chilly with the
near approach of autumn. But Tom took no notice of any of
them, though one and another who had grown familiar with
his face in the market called to him to come and join them. He
made his way as quickly as he could to the man whom he was
seeking. He found him very busy, and surrounded by customers;
but Tom had dealt with him for more than a year, and he had
found no reason to doubt his honesty. So, when he laid down
the money close to his hand, saying it was six-and-threepence
owing to him, the greengrocer dropped it at once into his bag,
with some other money which he had just received, and told
Tom it was all right.

All right! So Tom thought, as he turned away with a lighter
spirit, feeling that it was all right for him to be saved the loss of
the half-crown. Poor Tom! It was quite fair, he said to himself,
Mr. Mandsby should have looked more sharply at the money,
and his loss was his own fault. The next day he entered the
Savings Bank office again with a good five-shilling piece, and
put it safely with the rest of his riches, telling the clerk that the
shop-keeper in Downing Street had readily changed it for him;
and when he received his book back there was entered upon its
columns the sum of seven pounds and five shillings. He heard
no more of the bad half-crown; and he considered himself very
lucky and very clever to have got rid of it so quietly. Nor did his
conscience trouble him much; it was growing hard and seared,
and though he trembled and was afraid if any danger approached

him, so long as everything was smooth and safe, his conscience slumbered peacefully. It seemed "all right" to Tom.

All this while little Phil was going on well at school. The sharp starved lines had all vanished from his face, and it looked all the more beautiful for the rosy color which came into his pale cheeks. He was a favorite with the other boys, and, strange to say, with the master and mistress also. But Phil had winning ways, and just as he had always been successful in begging half-pence, or selling fusees, when he and Tom had snatched a scanty living off the streets, so now he won the love of all about him, and was happy in his new home. But the happiest days of all were when he had a holiday to spend in Pilgrim Street, and Tom, hastening over his work, came back early in the afternoon, bringing with him some delicacy to add to the feast which Alice always tried to provide upon that occasion. Phil could read and write better than Tom by this time, and Polly had got on well at her day-school; so now it was the custom for them to read a chapter round, verse by verse, while Nat sat by with Suey on his knee, listening with heart-felt delight. Those were happy days both in Tom's life and Phil's.

One of these delightful feasts was to be held on Michaelmas Day,[1] and Tom was desirous to get all his customers served early, so as to be in time to call for Phil in the afternoon, and give him a ride in the donkey-cart. He was going to make known publicly to them all his cherished scheme about the new cart which would involve the confession of what a large sum of money he possessed; and he felt all the importance of the coming event. How Nat Pendlebury would laugh! And how wide Alice's eyes would open! Tom laughed to himself at the very thought of it, and over and over again he rehearsed what he would say, and fancied he was laying down his Savings Bank book upon the table before

1 Michaelmas Day—a church festival held on the 29th of September.

their very eyes, to prove that he was not jesting with them. He played with the key of his box, which lay safely in his waistcoat-pocket; for he had a strong box of his own now, and a second suit of clothes, and he was always very careful to keep it well locked—for did not his valuable book lie at the bottom of it?

He was indulging in his pleasant forethoughts, when a servant beckoned to him from a door at hand, and asked him to weigh half a score pounds of potatoes. The price for them was sixpence, and, as she thought, she put a shilling into his hand, asking him to give her six pennies in copper for change. Tom glanced at the money, and up into the girl's face. She was in a hurry, she said, for she had to go to the butcher's shop, and she held out her hand for the change. Almost before Tom could count the six pennies into it she ran away, and he went on with his cart, looking again and again at the piece of money, which he held lovingly in his hard hand—for it was a bright and glittering sovereign!

How beautiful it looked in the sunshine, as Tom's eyes gloated upon it! And how speedy he was getting round the corner of the next street! He dared not cry his fruit and vegetables as usual, until he was sure he was out of the girl's hearing. If he should only be as lucky now as he was over the bad half-crown, he would have a whole pound to put into the Bank. He rubbed it, and breathed upon it, and rubbed it again; and he grew so engrossed in the occupation that his donkey began to lag, and he was not conscious of his reverie, until he heard a girl's voice calling him in loud and excited tones. Tom slipped the sovereign into his waistcoat-pocket, and then he turned to face the breathless girl.

"I gave you a sovereign just now," she gasped, "in mistake, instead of a shilling."

"Oh, no, miss," answered Tom, earnestly; "I looked at it when you gave it me, and it was no more than a shilling; and I gave you six coppers in change."

"I know you gave me six coppers," she said, pressing her hand upon her heart, and still panting for breath; "but missis gave me a sovereign and a shilling—the sovereign for the butcher, and the shilling for potatoes; and when I reached the butcher's I'd only got the shilling. I gave you the sovereign."

"No, you didn't, indeed, miss," replied Tom, opening his money-bag. "Look here! There isn't a sovereign amongst them, and I put all my money in here. I couldn't have taken it without knowing it."

"But you must have it," persisted the girl; "who else can have got it? I came right out of the house with the money, and I'd only that one shilling and one sovereign. You just give it up at once, there's a good lad, and I'll say no more about it."

"I can't give it up, if I haven't got it, can I?" asked Tom, angrily. "I've shown you my money-bag. I can't waste my time here all day. You just leave go of my cart."

"I won't," said the girl. "Police, please, you just come here, will you?"

A policeman had come up, unseen by Tom, and now, when he looked round, he quailed with fear as he saw Banner standing beside his donkey-cart. He was too frightened to see that Banner looked less stern than usual, for only the night before the lad had been the most attentive of his class. The girl told her tale hurriedly, and Tom repeated his denial with an oath, which escaped his lips in the confusion of the moment. Banner frowned, and his eye rested severely upon him.

"Thomas Haslam!" he uttered, in a tone which caused Tom to tremble from head to foot.

"I haven't got it," he cried, with another oath. "You may look in my money-bag, Mr. Banner. There's no such thing as a sovereign in it."

Banner stood silent for a minute, looking at the boy with a

feeling of real sorrow. Such pains he had taken with him, and such an interest he had felt in him! He had looked well after him, and taught him diligently; thinking he was doing Christian work, and was fulfilling his duty as a Christian man. In his own stiff and stern manner he had really felt a friendship for Tom, and pushed him forward in his business. And now it was come to this! For that one minute he was full of sorrow and disappointment; the next he was a policeman again, and his sole thought was to fulfil his duty as a policeman.

"Thomas Haslam," he said, "I must see what you have in your pockets, as well as your money-bag." In the old days Tom had had many a narrow escape from the hands of the police. In the confusion and excitement of the moment former habits resumed their hold upon him. The instinct of the City Arab to escape from a policeman, which had long slumbered but was not quite dead, revived. Reason and conscience were paralyzed by sudden terror at the certainty of detection. He glanced round, and saw a passage close at hand leading into a street beyond, and if he could only gain it he would have a good chance of getting off. Gathering up all his strength, he ran at Banner with his head, butting against him, and before the policeman could recover himself, or the girl lay hands upon him, he fled down the passage, and was lost to sight.

It was at first like a welcome return to the old wild, lawless life; and for a few minutes the only feeling Tom had was one of triumphant daring, and clever dodging of his old enemy, a policeman. He darted down many a short cut and narrow alley, till he was safe in the heart of the city; and then he hid himself in the doorway of an untenanted warehouse, to get his breath again after his rapid and successful flight. But he had not time to tarry long, for Banner would be on his track quickly. Then all at once, like a sudden burst of light which did not pass away in a flash, there came into his mind the utter and complete folly of his sin. True, he had possessed himself of a sovereign; but what had he lost? He had banished himself from Manchester, for he must flee at once, or be arrested as a thief, and be imprisoned, for how long he could not tell. He must leave behind him the business he had got together, and his stock in trade, and his box containing all his clothes, and more precious still, his Savings Bank book. At the thought of his Savings Bank book he clenched his teeth, and swore savagely at his own folly and wickedness. He dared not return to his lodgings, lest Banner should be there already. Every policeman would soon be on the look-out for him, and they knew him very well. There was only one way of escape now open to him. He was not far from Victoria Station, and trains were leaving there frequently for Liverpool. He had made himself a vagabond and beggar again by his own foolishness, and he must banish himself from all the old familiar streets, the only places he had known all his life long. Little Phil, too—but at the thought of little Phil Tom felt as if his heart would break. How little Phil and Alice would grieve and sorrow over him, and at first refuse to believe that he was guilty! But time was too precious for him to waste it in vain regrets. Very cautiously, with many backward glances lest Banner should be dogging his footsteps, he stole his way to the station, and paying for his ticket out of the sovereign which had been so great a temptation and curse to him, he got into the train for Liverpool.

Chapter 10

TOM'S FRIENDS

By the time Banner had recovered from the unexpected assault made upon him he knew that it would be quite useless to pursue Tom. He had the cart upon his hands too, and it could not be left in the middle of a street. The girl burst into a storm of rage and tears, for she knew she had lost the money partly by her own carelessness, and she was afraid her mistress would require her to make it good. Banner hesitated as to what course he should pursue. Stern and self-satisfied as he was, his heart melted towards poor Tom; and he found, strangely enough, a misgiving spring up in his mind as to whether he had really taken the best way to teach and befriend him. Maybe, if he had unbent a little more to the lad, been a little less of a police-man and a little more of a friend, Tom might not have taken flight, as if surprised by a foe. He scarcely knew what to do. The strict letter of his duty, perhaps, required him to accuse Tom of theft at the police-station, and have him arrested and thrown into jail for his crime, the very misery and calamity from which Mr. Hope had rescued him a little more than a twelvemonth ago. Banner had been acquainted with Mr. Hope for years, and he knew well what a bitter disappointment it would be to him to see Tom once again at the bar before the judge. Suppose he tried to screen and save the boy, and give him once more a chance of overcoming his early vices? Besides, Banner had been boastful of Tom's reformation, and talked of it to Mr. Watson and Mrs. Worthington; and now he felt it would be a sore mortification to himself to be compelled to give up his favorite scholar. All these motives together, pity for Tom, a doubt of his own instructions, the reluctance to disappoint Mr. Hope, and the mortification to himself, proved strong enough to conquer Banner's rigid sense of his duty as a policeman. The girl was crying beside the cart for the loss of the money chiefly, and she cared for little else; she had no very vengeful feelings against the thief, nor any strong desire for justice. Banner counted up the money in Tom's bag, which he still held in his hand, and found it contained twelve shillings and five pence, which he gave to the servant, promising to bring her the rest in the evening; and then he commissioned a man whom he knew to take the donkey-cart home to Tom's lodgings, with a message that he would see him after six o'clock. After which Banner went on his beat, thoughtful and grieved, but not relentless towards the unhappy castaway who had fallen back into his old sins.

By this time all the preparations for keeping Phil's holiday were completed in Pilgrim Street; but today they were unusually poor and scanty, for Nat Pendlebury had crushed his foot badly, and had been away from work for a fortnight; and Alice was secretly hoping that Tom would bring a good share to the enter-tainment. Phil arrived early, and was received with great demon-strations of welcome from the little ones and from Nat himself, who sat in Alice's rocking-chair in the chimney-corner. The twi-light, or rather the night—for it was always twilight in the cel-lar—seemed to fall earlier than usual, yet Tom did not come; so Phil and Joey went to his lodgings to see after him. They returned with mysterious and alarming intelligence; for the donkey-cart, with its store of fruit and vegetables, had been brought back by a stranger, who knew nothing of what had become of Tom, and had only said that Mr. Banner had told him to leave it there, with word that he would see Tom after six o'clock.

A strange uncomfortable gloom came over all the party. Nat could not understand what this news foreboded; and Alice set the bread upon the table, and made the weak tea in the tin teapot, with a sad expression upon her face. What in the world could have happened to Tom? Was he hurt, and taken to the infirmary? If father could have walked he might have gone to ask Mr. Banner; but she could not go very well, for she did not know where he lived, and she did not like to inquire at the police-station. The tea passed off in dull quietness, except that, at every step along the pavement above the window, they started with expectation, and little Phil ran to the door to look out for Tom. He would be too late if he did not come soon, as Phil must be back at school at seven o'clock. It was getting on fast for seven when they heard a measured stride up the street, and a sharp rap at the door, which made every one jump from their seats, except Nat, and before Alice could reach it, it was opened wide, and Banner entered. He looked round keenly, and fastened his eyes on the many-colored screen which partitioned off part of the cellar, as if he could see through it; after which he gazed severely, first at Nat, and then at Alice, till they felt quite uneasy under his scrutiny.

"Where is Thomas Haslam?" he asked, in a stern voice.

"That's just what we were going to ask you, Mr. Banner," said Nat; "little Phil and Joey have been asking after him at his lodgings, and the old folks say he's not come home, but you sent a man with his donkey-cart and all his stuff, a good four hours since. I humbly hope there's nothing amiss with poor Tom, Mr. Banner."

"Nathaniel Pendlebury," answered Banner, drily, "I'm inclined to be a true friend to Thomas, if he'll only come forward and confess his sin, and make restitution. Restitution I must insist upon, Nathaniel Pendlebury. If he's within hearing, he may reckon upon me being a friend, and not a policeman, to him."

"But Tom isn't within hearing," said Nat, in great anxiety; "if you mean he's behind the screen you are staring at, Mr. Banner, I say he hasn't been nigh us all day, though it is Phil's holiday and all. If you know anything about Tom, good or bad, please let us hear it at once."

Even Banner felt sure that Nat was telling him the simple truth, and that Tom could not be concealed behind the screen. Little Phil pressed up to him, and stood eager-eyed to hear any news of Tom; but Alice went pale, and Nat looked very downcast. In a few brief words Banner told them the occurrence of the day, and how Tom had made his escape, adding that he had just been to his lodgings, and could hear nothing of him.

Nat wrung his hands together, and Alice sank down upon the old stool, which had been placed ready for Tom, drawing little Phil towards her.

"Oh, Tom! Tom!" cried Nat; "poor Tom! This is worse than crushing my foot. What can we do for him, Mr. Banner? We mustn't let him fall back to the bad altogether again. I love the lad; but maybe we haven't done the best we could for him."

"I think I have," said Banner; but he spoke doubtfully. "I have taught him to read and write, and made him learn the commandments off by heart, and his duty towards God, and towards his neighbor; and I've made him understand that God Almighty will surely judge him and punish him, even for the smallest sin. He's gone wrong because he is bad through and through. He'll be a thief like his father."

"Oh, no, no!" cried little Phil, falling down on his knees beside Alice. "Please God, save Tom from being a thief! Please

God, take care of Tom wherever he is tonight, and bring him home again, and make him a good boy: for Jesus Christ's sake. Amen."

"Amen," echoed Nat; and Alice laid her hands upon Phil's curly hair, leaning her face upon them, and Phil felt her tears falling upon his forehead. They were very sad at heart for Tom, and even Banner, when he said he would see Phil safe home to school, took his little hand in his and pressed it tenderly, almost marvelling at himself for feeling so grieved and disappointed about a poor thief like Thomas Haslam.

The next morning Banner received a letter from Tom, scrawled upon a blank leaf torn out of his Bible which he had happened to have with him in his pocket. It had been posted at Victoria Station before he started, and was very short, but Banner had some difficulty in making it out.

"Mr. Banner, I kant surve God. I'm a wickid boy and a theef. I'm sory I hirt you. Plese give my luv to litle Phil, and Mis Alice, and Mister Nat. I'm going to be a wikid man, and never see enny of yu agen. So no more. I no God seese me. Thomas Haslam."

It seemed plain from this letter that Tom had fled from Manchester, lest he should be arrested and imprisoned for theft. But though the lad was a thief, Banner felt a tear dimming his sharp eye, which had to be wiped away before he could catch sight of the next criminal. He would not charge the theft upon Tom, and set the police on his track, so he paid the rest of the sovereign out of his own pocket to the servant, and took upon himself to give Tom's stock of fruit and vegetables to the Pendleburys. He also took possession of Tom's box, and had it conveyed to the house where he himself lodged, after giving a paper to the care of Nat Pendlebury, stating that he had done so in order that it might be safe for Tom if he should ever come back to claim it.

Chapter 11

A MESSAGE FROM HEAVEN

Tom's mind was all confusion and bewilderment as the train carried him away from all the familiar haunts of Manchester to the strange town of Liverpool. His first fear was lest any of his fellow-passengers should guess his crime, and give him up at one of the stations where the train stopped. As soon as this fear was lulled, then sprung up the dread of a railway accident, such as he had heard of, in which he might be crushed to death, and so be hurried to the judgment-seat of his angry God. He had never been such a journey before, and a man who sat beside him was talking of all the terrible accidents he could remember, until Tom was thrilling through and through with terror. Once the long shrill whistling of the engine caused him to start from his seat, and endeavour to cast himself through the door of the carriage, but his fellow-travellers held him back, with many expressions of anger and scorn at his terrified rashness. At last they reached Liverpool, and Tom found himself alone and friendless, loitering upon the pavement outside the station, with houses and streets all around him; but how different from the streets of Manchester! He did not know where to turn, but after a while he dragged himself away, and stealing guiltily along the broad and handsome streets, he at last entered into a labyrinth of strange alleys, where every face was the face of a stranger. How long it seemed already since he had stolen the sovereign from the servant! And yet only this morning he had started off to his work with a glad and lightsome heart, looking forward to seeing little Phil.

It never entered into Tom's head that he should be at any loss in finding means to earn his own living. He was better off than when Mr. Hope had given him his first start in life, for he had a decent suit of clothes, and a good pair of boots, besides the money in his pocket, of which he had spent only two shillings and seven pence in buying his railway ticket. All the rest was his to set up in business again; and he had nothing to do but to repeat his life as he had passed it during the last eighteen months. For Tom was resolved not to steal again, but to work hard, and save as before. He went early in the morning to the market, and made his purchases as carefully as in the Shude Hill market at home; but he had not taken into account that he did not know in what direction to bend his steps, and he lost several days in wandering about the suburbs of the town in search of a neighborhood where he could sell his stock. Moreover, sharp as he was, Tom found the Liverpool rogues sharper than himself, and he was cheated of his money, cheated every way, until, at the end of a fortnight, he found himself without a penny in his pocket.

Then there began a harder struggle for bare life than even Tom, in the worst days of his misery, had ever experienced. One by one he exchanged his good clothes for the merest rags; and by-and-bye he was brought down to spending his nights anywhere that he could find the least shelter from the severity of the weather, or wherever the police would suffer him to lie still in peace. He had known want, and cold, and starvation in former times, but never such wretchedness as now; for when everything else failed, little Phil could always get a few crusts or a penny or two by begging. He could not even find a chance of stealing any food, though he hung about the bakers' shops for hours together, for it seemed as though suspicious eyes were upon him everywhere, and the policemen dogged his steps, and bade him move on whenever he loitered upon his miserable wanderings. Now and then people a little less poverty-stricken than himself gave him some work to do, and paid him in coarse food, so that life was just kept within his starved and shrivelled body. Homeless, in rags, famished, too big for begging, and too keenly watched for thieving, poor Tom was reaping the harvest of his sin and folly; while Nat and Alice Pendlebury, and little Phil, and Banner the policeman, were praying every day to the Father in heaven to keep him safe, and to bring him home again.

Thus day after day Tom sank lower and lower into the great gulf of wretchedness, until he looked back with longing and regret to the time when he had been sheltered in a jail, and waiting to be brought before the judge. One day he rallied all his failing courage, and threw a stone at a shop-window, hoping that he would be taken to prison for it; but for once there was no policeman at hand, and the shop-keeper caught him, flogged him severely, and then bade him begone. Tom slank away with bruised shoulders, and a crushed spirit. Altogether broken, and trodden down, and cast away, with a feeble body and a wretched soul, the days dragged slowly past for him, and the long wintry nights, with their thick fogs from the sea, wrapped about him their chilly darkness. He had neither hope nor strength. Yet one night, as he crouched under some bales upon the landing stage,[1] gazing out with his sunken eyes upon the black waves, glimmering here and there beneath the solitary lamps in the poops[2] of the vessels, there came across his brain a strange memory. It was

1 Landing stage—a floating dock to load and unload goods and passengers.
2 Poop—the highest part of the rear deck of a ship.

almost as if some still and quiet voice were whispering to him, and it said these words: "He that overcometh shall inherit all things; and I will be his God, and he shall be My son."

ON THE LANDING STAGE.

Chapter 12

BACK TO PILGRIM STREET

t was a great grief to the Pendleburys that Tom should have turned out so badly after all; but they had other troubles of their own, which swallowed up their sorrow for him. The doctor said that Nat's foot would never be strong enough for him to take to his old laborious work again; and he did not know what business he could turn to, to earn a living for himself and his children. Kitty was earning six shillings a week at the mill, but what was that among so many? Banner and he talked the matter over many a time, but they could not strike any light which might shine into the obscure future. In the meantime they just managed to live. Alice was a good worker, and Banner obtained two or three days' work every week for her, with people whom he knew. There were also unexpected gifts sent in, a few pounds of flour or oatmeal, or loaves of bread, from nobody knew where, except Banner, who felt himself growing very soft-hearted, and took every precaution against the Pendleburys' finding out who was their unknown benefactor; for he had always set his face against alms-giving, and there was not a policeman in the borough more strict against beggars.

But before the depth of winter came, the good turn which Nat had been hoping for arrived. Phil told Mrs. Worthington

the whole story of their distress, and she procured for Nat the
post of night-watchman in her husband's mill, where Kitty
worked. The duties were not heavy, and Nat, even with his lame
foot, would be quite equal to them, especially with the aid of a
good dog. He had never been of a drowsy turn, he said to Mrs.
Worthington; six hours' sleep was more than enough to set him
up for the rest of the twenty-four; and it did not matter a straw
at what time he had his short slumber. Anybody could see that
Nat was too brisk, and lively, and wiry to be caught napping;
and as to his honesty and trustworthiness, there was many a
citizen of Manchester who would readily give him a first-rate
character.

The Pendleburys felt that their fortune was made, as indeed
it was, for Nat was to receive a pound a week; and Alice no longer looked forward to the bitter frosts and deep snows of winter
with anxiety. But for the absence of Tom, and the fretting of little Phil, they would have been perfectly happy in Pilgrim Street.

There was still another friend of Tom's, to whom his down-
fall and disappearance were a great grief. Banner had been
obliged to endure the mortification of owning himself at fault as
to Tom's reformation, both to Mr. Watson and Mrs. Worthington; but that was little compared to the reluctance he felt in
telling Mr. Hope about it, when he came at the beginning of
the year to spend a few days with his sister. It was more than
three months now since Tom's flight, and not a word had been
heard from him, though Banner had made many private inquiries from the police force in other towns about him. Mr. Hope
was disappointed as well as troubled. He had fancied that he saw
in the boy such signs of a desire to be good, and to learn what
was good, as gave a fair promise that he would grow up a really
Christian man, loving God as his Father, and trusting in the
Lord Jesus Christ as his Saviour and Friend. Whenever he had

spoken anything about this happy belief, Tom's eyes had grown soft with tears, and his lips had trembled with a sob, and though he had said nothing, there had been a look of wonder and gladness upon his face, as if a new and happy thought of God had found an entrance into his heart. He accompanied Banner to Pilgrim Street to consult with Nat about Tom; for these three men, in their own way, were true friends to the lost lad, and they considered it worth their while to arrange some plan for seeking him out, and saving him from continued crime, if it were possible.

It was getting on for six o'clock, the hour when the night-watchman was expected to be upon duty, before their consultation was finished; and Mr. Hope and Banner said they would go as far as the mill with Nat Pendlebury. The nearest cut was by the cathedral, and through the narrow bye-street where Tom had long ago found a quiet corner for contemplating his new bright sovereign. The day had been very cold and dreary; snowing and thawing, and freezing and snowing again. So much of the sky as could be dimly seen over the houses was full of snow-clouds; and under foot the pavement was partly ice and partly plashes of snow and mud. The points of the doorways and casements were all white with frost, and along every street which lay open to the north and east there came biting blasts of wind which seemed to sting through the thickest clothing. Nobody was out of doors who could help it. It was no time for talking, said Mr. Hope; they would get to the mill, and once within its shelter they could talk with comfort.

They were walking briskly along in single file past the cathedral, Banner being first with his lantern, when he almost fell over a figure, which was half lying and half kneeling against the wall. He turned the full blaze of his lamp upon it; and there lay a miserable, shrivelled, meagre wretch, scarcely covered by his rags, and with a face white and starved, but partly hidden by the matted hair. It looked dead, this pale and withered face, and the thin hands were stiff and frozen; but as Banner stooped down, and pushed the hair away from the cold forehead, he cried in a voice of trouble and alarm, "Why, look here, Mr. Hope, and Nat! It's Tom!"

Yes. It was no other than Tom, who had at last crawled back home to die, as he thought. How he had made his way from Liverpool, he could never clearly remember; but step after step along the weary road he had dragged his failing feet homewards, until at length his dim eyes caught sight of the tall chimneys of Manchester lying in the distance before him, and the sight gave him heart to struggle on. With untold pain and toil, he had crept over the icy pavements with his naked feet, until at nightfall he found himself once more under the cathedral walls, and only a short run from Pilgrim Street in the old times. For it was to Pilgrim Street he was going home; and if he could only reach the door, and see the light of the fire burning within, and maybe hear the sound of voices reading, or singing, round the warm hearth, he thought he could bear even to die, though he must go and face his Judge after death. But, as he sat down for a few minutes to rest himself, and gather strength, the chimes of the clock in the tower above him struck one quarter of an hour after another, until he felt as if his life were slowly dying away, like the faint smouldering of some fire which is nearly extinguished; and with a feeble and bitter groan of despair he sank down on the frozen stones, and knew nothing more.

Mr. Hope, and Banner, and Nat Pendlebury stood round Tom, and for a minute or two none of them could speak a word for surprise and dread. Then Nat knelt down beside him, and laid his hand upon his breast, and put his cheek to the parted lips. There was a faint fluttering still in the lad's heart; and as

THE RETURN OF THE RUNAWAY.

soon as Banner heard that he was alive he gave his lantern to
Mr. Hope, and lifted the poor starved, stunted frame from the
ground. He must carry Tom to Pilgrim Street, said Nat, for it
was nigh at hand, and Alice was a capital nurse; so they retraced
their steps to Nat's cellar, while Mr. Hope went a different way
to fetch a doctor. Tom's consciousness came back for a moment
or two, and he felt himself being borne gently along in some
man's strong arms, with a warm coat wrapped round him; but
he could neither speak nor look up, only it seemed very pleasant, and Banner heard a feeble gasp from his lips, which made
his own heart throb with a strange delight.

All night long, in Nat Pendlebury's cellar, Banner watched
like a woman beside Tom, feeding him at short intervals under
the doctor's directions, and striving to bring back life to him.
Nat was obliged to attend to his duties as night-watchman, and
Mr. Hope went away after learning that there was no immediate danger. So Banner had the charge of Tom chiefly to himself,
and as the quiet hours passed by, and he watched the gradual
strengthening of returning life in his death-like face, and saw
him at last sink into a safe and healthful slumber, a new and
deeper tenderness for the poor boy took possession of his soul.

It was nearly a week before Tom was strong enough to get
out of bed and sit on the hearth, with the screen put between
him and the door, that no cold draught should by chance blow
upon him. Phil had leave to have a holiday; and Nat Pendlebury,
with a little hesitation, ventured to take the liberty of inviting
Mr. Banner to drink a cup of tea with them. For a moment Banner was staggered; but he had grown very familiar with all the
Pendleburys during the last few days, and after a slight pause of
consideration he accepted Nat's invitation. Alice felt somewhat
nervous at first, and Nat was very ceremonious in his hospitality; but the policeman set them all at ease, and even insisted

upon taking Joey on his knee as soon as tea was over, and they gathered round the hearth with the light of the blazing fire shining upon their faces, while on the table behind a candle was burning uselessly, out of compliment to Mr. Banner. Not Nat's face alone, but every face beamed with gladness, except Tom's, which was still white and listless, and still bore many sorrowful lines traced there during his months of wretched wandering.

Alice knew it, and Banner suspected it, but nobody else thought for a moment that Mr. Hope intended to come and see them that night, to bid Tom good-bye; for he was to leave Manchester the next morning, and would not come back till the assizes. But even Alice was taken by surprise, for Mrs. Worthington came with him, looking as pleasant as if she were visiting some grand lady in a handsome drawing-room. She had to have Alice's rocking-chair, and Nat gave Mr. Hope his seat, and there they sat as comfortably and as much at home, to all appearance, as if there had been a Brussels carpet on the floor, and steel bars to the grate.

"Tom," said Mr. Hope, after a while, "can you tell us now what you've been doing all this time?"

"Oh, no!" answered Tom; "I'm a wicked boy, and a thief, and all of you are so good," and he buried his face in his hands, and wept very bitterly.

"Tom," said Mr. Hope, in a voice that was full of comfort, "do you remember that verse I gave you to learn in your Bible?"

"Ay," answered Tom, with a great sob, "it was that brought me home again. I thought somebody was whispering it to me all the while, and all along the road. But I can't overcome. I can't serve God."

"None of us can serve God till we become His children in Christ Jesus," said Mr. Hope; "as long as we think of Him as a hard master, we shall never serve Him, or overcome our own sins. We are to know Him not only as our King, or our Judge, or our Master, but as our Father who is in heaven. Only when we feel that God is truly our Father, through Jesus our Saviour, shall we have power to overcome our sins. You would not like to grieve and offend a father who was loving and taking care of you all the while, Tom?"

"But how can God be my father?" asked Tom, lifting up his pale face, and gazing earnestly at Mr. Hope.

All the rest were looking at him, as if they were asking the same question, and he smiled and said in a solemn and quiet voice, "He came unto His own, but His own received Him not. But as many as received Him, to them gave He power to become the sons of God even to them that believe on His name."[1]

"That's it!" cried Nat; "the Lord Jesus gives us the power to become the children of God. He knew what it was to be the Son of God, and what a place heaven was, so He came down to die for us, and to give us strength, and to take away all our sins. Ay, without Him we can do nothing. Bless you, without Him I couldn't overcome the smallest sin! Tom, my boy, if thee wants to be God's son, and to overcome, and to inherit all things, you must just believe on the Lord Jesus, and all He says to us in the Bible. Thee'lt serve God then sure enough."

"I'm so wicked," murmured Tom; "I've more to overcome than any of you."

"The Lord himself had to overcome," said Mr. Hope; "in all things He was made like unto His brethren—for He calls us brethren, Tom—and He was tempted in all points like as we are, and suffered being tempted, so that He knows all about us, and is able to help them that are tempted. You have suffered nothing that your Savior has not suffered before you. You have many things to overcome—sin, and poverty, and sickness, and

1 John 1:11–12.

ignorance; but Christ knows all, and He died on the cross that His blood might wash away all our sin. He will give you power to become one of the sons of God, out of all your wretchedness and sin. He says, 'To him that overcometh will I grant to sit with Me on My throne, even as I also overcame, and am set down with My Father on His throne.'[1] When you are sitting with Christ on His throne, Tom, you will look down upon all this great misery, and thank Him for helping you to overcome it."

For a few minutes there was silence in the room, while Tom sat thinking, with his thin hands clasping Phil's, who knelt on the hearth beside him; but all at once a change came over his sad face, as if some bright light from heaven beamed upon it; his eyes sparkled though they were filled with tears, and his hungry lips melted into a smile. He looked like a slave, who had just escaped from bondage, and was flinging his heavy yoke and slavish chains behind him.

"Ah," he cried, "I was afraid of God! He always seemed angry, and I'd no heart to serve Him. But the Lord Jesus loved me and died for me, and He will help me to keep His commandments, and do my duty to God, and my duty to my neighbor. Jesus won't mind me having been a thief, and the son of a thief, will He, sir?"

Mr. Hope took up Tom's Bible, which lay on the table near at hand, and he read aloud from it these words, while Tom listened eagerly to them:

"And one of the thieves which were hanged railed on Him, saying, If Thou be the Christ, save Thyself and us.

"But the other answering rebuked him, saying, Dost not thou fear God, seeing thou art in the same condemnation?

"And we indeed justly; for we receive the due reward of our deeds; but this man hath done nothing amiss.

---

1 Revelation 3:21.

"And he said unto Jesus, Lord, remember me when Thou comest into Thy kingdom.

"And Jesus said unto him, Verily, I say unto thee, today shalt thou be with Me in Paradise."[1]

---

1 Luke 23:42–43.

Chapter 13

AN UNWELCOME RE-APPEARANCE

I t was a new life that Tom had entered upon. All the old dark, dreary, solitary life, in which he had neither friend nor father, was ended for ever; and now when he lay down upon his hard flock bed at night, or opened his eyes to the dim light of the cellar in the morning, there was a calm, peaceful satisfaction in his heart as he thought of God. What did it matter that he was poor and weakly, stricken into the profound depths of poverty and sickness, when he had the assurance in his own spirit that, feeble and cast down as he was with many old sins in the past, and many temptations in the present, he was still one of God's sons, and the Lord Jesus Christ was as truly his elder brother as he was brother to little Phil. Tom knew very little more than this of the good news which the Saviour of the world came to bring. He knew next to nothing of the many parables and teachings of the Lord, nor of His miracles, and the mighty works which He did; and he had never read any of the epistles, written by the disciples of Christ after His death, for the instruction of those who believed on Him through their words. He was as unlearned and simple in the gospel of Christ as the little child who can only totter to his father's knee, and look up into his face, and try to lisp the word "Father." This was all the boy could do, but he did it trustfully, and with all his heart. He looked up into the face of God, and his stammering tongue cried, "My Father, which art in heaven!"

What a change it made in him, and in all about him! He loved the Pendleburys with a new affection, and their home was yet more the pleasantest place in the world for him. But he was well enough now to begin to work for his own living again, for he must no longer be burdensome to Nat and Alice, though they put him off for a day or two when he first spoke of leaving them, and returning to his old den of a sleeping-place. But he knew what it would be his duty to do. He asked Banner to bring him his Savings Bank book out of the box of which he had taken the charge, and the first time he was able to leave Pilgrim Street alone he crawled feebly along the crowded pavement, with his wan face and trembling limbs, a very skeleton of famine, as far as the Post-Office, where he gave in his book, and a warrant which had been sent to him from the office in London, to enable him to take out all his savings. He thought he should need them all; for he must pay Banner the money he had given out of his own pocket to the servant girl, to make up the sovereign he had stolen; and there was the bad half-crown to be made good to the greengrocer in Shude Hill market; and there was the doctor who had attended him so frequently; and he ought to pay Nat and Alice well for their care and kindness towards him. If there should be anything to spare after all these claims were settled, he must use it to start in business again. The clerk gave him what seemed almost a handful of glittering coins, seven golden sovereigns, and four silver shillings; and there was a chink and tinkle in the sound as he gathered them into his hand which would have sounded as sweet as music in his ears only six months ago. But just then came that whisper, whether in his heart or not he scarcely knew, saying, "Our Father!" and the smile that shone upon his poor pale face had nothing at all to do with the money. The love of money was swallowed up in the love of God.

Tom was retracing his steps slowly and weariedly to Pilgrim Street, when he heard Alice's voice calling behind him, and turning round he saw her hurrying along to overtake him. She wanted him to lean upon her strong arm homewards, but Tom hesitated. She looked so trim and tidy in her clean print gown, and her black straw bonnet, and her dark shawl; and he was so ragged and tattered, still wearing the clothes in which he had returned to Manchester, that he felt it would be an unsightly thing for him to be seen leaning upon her. But before he could speak Alice had drawn his hand through her arm, and was walking with slow and steady steps at his side.

"Why, Tom," she asked, cheerfully, "whatever has thee got wrapped up so tight in thy hand? A banknote, maybe, by the way thee grips it?"

"Ay, Alice," answered Tom, "and more than a banknote. It's seven pound four shillings; all my savings afore I went to Liverpool. Mr. Banner knows all about it."

"Seven pound!" repeated Alice, in a tone of wonder; "why, it's a fortune, Tom. Seven pound four shillings! However, in all the world, did thee save all that money?"

There was time enough to tell Alice all about it, and what he intended to do with it, before they came in sight of the corner of Pilgrim Street. At this corner there stood a strong-limbed but elderly man, with grizzled hair, a face well marked with many lines and wrinkles, and with cunning eyes, which were looking keenly and eagerly about him. He was dressed in a coarse but decent suit of clothes, and over his shoulders hung a carpenter's satchel. But neither Alice nor Tom noticed him, so engrossed were they in their own conversation, until he seized Tom by the shoulder, and spoke in a voice which was loud and rough.

"Tom Haslam," he said; "thou'rt Tom Haslam!"

Tom started, as if awakened from a pleasant dream by some sudden shock, and with a feeling of terror he raised his eyes to the stranger's face. His remembrance of it was dim, but still he could recollect it with a shivering dread creeping through all his frame. He gripped Alice's arm, and leaned heavily upon it, for the little strength he had was forsaking him, and his feeble fingers loosed their hold of the little packet of money in his hand, and it fell to the pavement, while his white lips muttered the word "Father!"

"Ay, lad, father, sure enough," said the man, stooping to pick up the packet. "But, hello! what's this? Money, Tom! see thee now—money, and plenty of it! Is it thine, lad?"

Haslam turned the coins about, and clinked them together, while Tom was struggling to regain his breath and his voice; for at first the houses seemed to whirl before his eyes, and the sun had spun round in the misty sky. Alice was holding him up, or he felt as if he should sink down upon the ground at his father's feet. But at last he felt strong enough to loose his grasp of her, and to lay his hand beseechingly upon his father's arm.

"It is my savings; but it's not mine," he gasped. "I owe it all. Part to Mr. Banner, the policeman."

At the word policeman the man looked somewhat frightened, and Tom went on more readily.

"He made up a sovereign for me out of his own pocket," he said, "and I must pay it back; and there's a bad half-crown to be made good; and I must pay Mr. Pendlebury for being ill at his home. You must give the money back to me, father."

"Not I," said Haslam, putting it into his pocket, "not till thou's made a better tale out, my lad. I don't pick up money like dirt to do that, I promise thee. But who's this lass with thee? A decent lass, too!"

"I'm Alice Pendlebury," she answered, "and our house is close by, if thee likes to step in there to talk to Tom. All the neighbors will be coming out if we stand talking here. This way, please."

Tom followed Alice with tottering steps, and sank down exhausted into a chair as soon as he entered the house, while his father stood in the doorway turning over the money, and gazing upon it with delight. Alice was a little afraid of Tom's father, for she knew that he had been in jail for eight years; but she invited him civilly to come in, and set a chair for him near to Tom.

"Well, my lad," said Haslam, "art glad to see thy father again, eh? How thou's grown, but as thin as a whipping-post. Thou has been worse dealt with than me. Better follow in my steps, Tom. It's not such a bad do, after all's said and done, to get eight years' board and lodging for nothing."

But though Haslam laughed loudly, his face was dark and wrathful, and his mirth was flat and spiritless. Tom's eyes were fastened upon him, and he could not turn them away. He had so long dreaded the release of his father, that now the calamity had suddenly befallen him he had no power either to think or to speak. Alice too was very quiet; and at length Haslam, growing uneasy under Tom's fascinated gaze, broke out with an oath—

"I'm thy father, as what else I am," he said; "and thou'lt have to own me, and obey me, or we'll see which is the strongest. Speak out, lad, art glad I'm let loose?"

"No," murmured Tom, almost in spite of himself, and Haslam laughed again, more loudly and harshly than before.

"A good son," he cried, "a very good son! I've a lesson or two to teach thee. And where's my other boy, little Phil?"

Alice was about to answer, for Tom's quivering lips seemed speechless, when with a great effort he sprang from his seat, and laid his hand eagerly upon hers, and as soon as he could command his voice he met his father's angry frown with a brave and steady gaze.

"Phil's safe and well, with good friends," he gasped, "but I'll not tell you where he is. Never! Not if thou beat me to death. Leave little Phil alone! he's being cared for. Oh, father, father, let Phil alone, for God's sake!"

"Well, well," said Haslam, "there's no hurry. I'll leave him alone for a day or two; but I must see my boys, both of them. Come, Tom, let's be friends, thee and me. This is a sorry welcome to give thy father after eight years. I mean to do well by thee. I'm a changed man, Tom; so the chaplain says, and it's his business to know. I'm all right now, my lad, and we're going to be decent folks now I reckon, thee and me."

There was a smile on Haslam's face which was not pleasant to see, but neither Tom nor Alice noticed it. They only heard his words, and a feeble hope sprang up in their hearts that there might be some truth in them. He said very soon afterwards that he must go and seek out a lodging, and if he found any that would do he would return to fetch Tom, for he was not going to be parted from his son again; and by-and-bye they would have little Phil at home with them. So saying, he took his departure, carrying away Tom's money with him. Not daring to speak a word, Tom and Alice watched him stride down Pilgrim Street, with his head held well up, as if he were as honest a man as any whom he could meet in the crowded city. Tom sank back into his chair again, and bent his face upon his hands.

"Oh!" he cried, "I wish I might never see his face again. I wish one of us was dead!"

"Hush, hush!" said Alice, in a soothing voice, "he is thy father, Tom; and maybe he is changed, as he says. The Lord Jesus didn't cast out the thief, and thee and me mustn't, Tom, must we? And remember, thou hast another Father, Tom."

Yes, he had another Father; but in the sharpness and suddenness of the trouble he felt himself averse to calling upon God by the same name which belonged to Haslam. "Father" had two sounds for Tom, one so full of gracious comfort, and of peace passing all understanding, that an hour ago he could not refrain from whispering it to himself over and over again. But the other sound was one of shame, and misery, and dread, and his lips trembled when he had to utter it aloud. Only an hour since his heart had seemed full of music and singing, as he looked up to the narrow strip of sky lying above the streets, and said, "Father!" But now the word that had been like a tone out of an angel's song had become a hateful and jarring sound. He sat still until he was rested a little; and then he strolled out again in a fever of disquietude and dismay into the bustling streets, where no quiet nook could be found in which he could get all alone and think. He longed for some secret peaceful place, but there was not any for a ragged boy like him; the police would not let him sit down upon a doorstep, and when he presented himself at the cathedral door, the verger bade him begone for a ragamuffin. At last he crept under the scaffolding reared about the tower of the cathedral, which was being rebuilt, and sat down on one of the great stones, which was to be placed in the massive masonry. It was noon-time, and the masons were gone to their dinner; and though a constant stream of people were passing to and fro before his eyes, yet he was alone in the cathedral enclosure. The sun shone down upon him with a mild warmth, and just overhead, where it was not clouded by mist or smoke, there was a patch of pale blue wintry sky. Tom scarcely knew why the sight quieted him, but he grew calmer and calmer in spirit, and at length, not joyously and buoyantly as before, but with a deeper and stronger feeling that it was true, he said in his heart, "I have another Father, my Father in heaven!"

Chapter 14

UPSIDE DOWN

aslam met with a room to let down a court in one of the streets lying at the back of the New Bailey, a jail with which he was well acquainted, though his long term of imprisonment had not been spent there. It was a good way from Pilgrim Street, especially while Tom was still so weakly; but that was no disadvantage in Haslam's eyes. Still he was quite desirous to stand well in Nat Pendlebury's opinion, and yet more so in Banner's, for he was out of jail with a ticket-of-leave for the two years which still remained of his sentence, and it was prudent to be on good terms with the police force. On that account he paid Tom's debt to Banner, and gave Alice a sovereign for her care of Tom during his illness. The rest of the money Tom saw nothing of; only he and his father lived upon dainties for a week or two, Haslam being a good cook, and very much inclined to make up for the plain diet of the jail from which he had been set free. Tom's strength came back very slowly; for the court in which they lived was close and over-crowded, and only the keenness of the east wind made the air at all fit to breathe. But these biting east winds were too cold for him to venture out, so he sat shivering beside the small fire, and reading his Bible diligently, while his father slept on a mattress in the corner, or smoked a pipe all

the day long, going out generally in the evening, for what purpose Tom did not dare to inquire, and coming back at four or
five o'clock in the morning.

There was one standing subject of contention between Tom
and his father, which threatened every day to break out into a
deadly quarrel. Haslam, for some reason or another, was bent
upon finding out Phil, and claiming him; and Tom felt that he
would sooner die than betray the refuge of his little brother. Nat
Pendlebury and Banner were also on their guard; and Haslam
found that neither force nor fraud could avail for the discovery
of the secret. He was, as I said, exceedingly anxious to avoid
awakening the suspicions of the policeman, and that proved a
great restraint upon him in his conduct towards Tom; so that to
the boy's great relief and surprise his life with his father was not
so hard a lot as he had dreaded. As he lost some of his fear, he
began to feel a little affection for him, and a hope that some day
or other he too might learn and believe the truths which he had
himself learned about God. Had he not himself been a thief?
Yet now, day after day, he could think of God as his heavenly
Father, and of Christ as his elder Brother, "the first-born among
many brethren;" and constantly, with slow but sure progress,
he was believing more and more in the infinite love and compassion of God towards all men, however vile their sins might
be. If then God loved his father, how much more ought he to
love him, and to honor him according to the commandment of
God, by rendering obedience to him in all things lawful. It was
only on the one point of telling where little Phil was that Tom
opposed his father's will, and he did that meekly, but with great
steadfastness.

As soon as he was able to work, Tom started off along his
old beat up Ardwick, with a basket of fish or vegetables upon
his head, for he could no longer hire a donkey-cart; and though

Banner once or twice deliberated whether he should advance him money enough to start again upon his former footing, he decided that it would be better to wait and see how Haslam conducted himself for a few months, for at present Tom's earnings would go to his father, and he had no intention of helping to keep an idle ticket-of-leave man. This same ticket-of-leave afforded a great hindrance to Haslam getting any regular employment. He seemed very much in earnest in trying to get work; yet in some way or other the secret was certain to ooze out, how Banner could never quite understand. Twice, when he was pretty sure of a place, Haslam himself told it frankly; and he lost the employment with a private chuckle of satisfaction, for he had no desire for constant and regular work, though he wished Banner to think so. Now and then he got a few odd jobs to do; and in the meantime he was never short of money to buy himself dainty food to eat, or intoxicating liquors to drink; though he did everything so quietly, that even Banner, with all his shrewdness, believed him to be as good a ticket-of-leave man as had ever come across his path. Still, for one reason or another, Banner hesitated about placing Tom into a larger way of business; and the boy toiled along, day after day, with a heavy basket upon his aching head, or upon his stooping shoulders, working bravely for the daily bread which he asked his heavenly Father to give to him. When he said, "Give us this day our daily bread," it did not enter his mind that he might sit idly by the fireside, and wait and see if it would drop down like the manna from heaven; but he shouldered his basket, and started off upon his work, through fair weather and foul weather, yet still acknowledging that it was God who gave to him that which he labored for.

But though Tom was as wishful as in the times that were gone by to serve his customers well, and to gain their good-will, and though Banner again spoke a good word for him here and

there, he had not the same success that had followed his labors
before. Partly because his extreme destitution, and long illness
in the depth of the winter, had made him so weak that often he
had to sit down to rest himself for half an hour at a time, and
partly because he could only carry about with him a small quan-
tity of the things which he sold, he could not now do more than
earn a bare living; for his father always expected him to pay his
share of the rent of the close, squalid, dirty room in which they
lived. For his food he could only buy the cheapest and coarsest
provisions, which contained very little nourishment; and sometimes, when his father was cooking his savory supper at the fire,
Tom felt even sharper pangs of appetite than he had done when
he was almost, dying of famine.

It was a hard thing, a bitter, sore temptation to discontent
and distrust, to sit aside in the dusky corner, where there was not
light enough to read his Bible, and with only a hard dry crust to
gnaw, while his father, with a face of enjoyment, devoured his
dainty food greedily, without once offering him a mouthful of
it. And Tom needed it so much; he felt it more and more every
day, as the keen cold east winds of the early spring stung him
through his thin clothing, and made good food more necessary
for reviving and keeping up his strength. It was a strange way
in which Tom was set to learn the love of God; but still, out of
his faintness, and hunger, and raggedness, he looked up to God,
and called him "Father."

Once he found time, and words as well, to let Nat Pendlebury see something of the thoughts that were filling his heart
with peace. They met on the broad flagged pavement before the
Royal Infirmary, where there are benches placed for the use of
any one who wishes to sit down and watch the central noise, and
stir, and tumult of the city. Nat had little Suey in his arms, and
was trotting up and down the pavement in the brief sunshine of

a March noontide, when Tom came wending his way weariedly
back from Ardwick, with his empty basket. He was very glad to
see Nat and to rest beside him on the lowest step of a statue of
the Duke of Wellington, which stands before the Infirmary—a
pale, pinched, stunted lad, never likely now to make a strong
and sturdy man, yet a conqueror as truly as the great soldier
above him; and the people who passed by saw him only as a
ragged beggar, but the angels in heaven, who had rejoiced over
his repentance, knew him as one of the sons of God.

"Mr. Pendlebury," said Tom, hesitatingly, "if God is like a
father, I wish every father 'ud be more like God."

"Ay, lad," answered Nat, pressing Suey's head down upon
his breast, "that's what I'm always asking Him. I'd like to be as
tender, and careful, and loving for the little ones, as He is for us.
Bless you, if I ever do have to say a sharp word it cuts me more
nor them; and I can't bear to think on it afterwards. I suppose
He feels something like that. He can't bear to have to punish,
only we're so fractious and contrary, and He's bound to do it."

"Dost think," said Tom, in a low voice, "that God really does
know what we have to eat and drink, and what clothes we have
on?"

"Ay, to be sure," said Nat, cheerily; "don't I know that Alice
has got a patch on her boot, and Polly wants a new frock, and
what we're going to have for dinner today? I should be nothing
of a father if I didn't take note of such like things; and if I didn't
cast about in my mind how they are all to be provided for. How
the Lord must cast about to provide for us all! He doesn't rain
us down bread from heaven, of course; we couldn't look to have
everything we want in that miraculous way. But He makes our
wants fit in one to another. Look here. I want a herring or two,
maybe, and thee wants to sell some herrings, so we come across
one another, and both of us get our wants provided for. Then

there's a girl wants a new gown, and a shopman wants to sell her a gown. And there's a man wanting matches, and a boy selling matches. That's how we fit in. Bless you, if the wisest man in the world, with the longest head, had to provide for the folks in Manchester, he'd be certain to forget lots of things. He'd forget matches, or chips, or tenpenny nails, or paste-pots, or something we could not do without; but the Lord has ordered it so that we all fit in together, and get along comfortably."

Nat's eyes fell upon Tom's pinched face, and he went on still more earnestly.

"Some things don't seem plain to understand," he said. "When I was a bill-sticker, it was very hard upon me not knowing how to read; and I never could learn, Tom. There's something wrong inside of my head, I reckon, for R and B always get wrong; and I never could remember which had the little curly twist through it, O or Q. So my wife used to tear off the right-hand top corner of all my bills, for fear I should post them upside down, and lose my business. But one night, when she was trusting to the fire-light, and we hadn't much fire, she tore off the wrong corner, the one right opposite to it, in the left-hand corner, thee knows. Well, the next morning out I went, and every bill I posted on the walls was upside down; and somehow I felt uneasy in my mind, and I stood and stared at each one after I'd done it, but I couldn't make it out. The reading didn't look right, but I couldn't tell for my ignorance; only I was uneasy. Ever since then, when things have looked uncomfortable and awkward, I've thought they were like the bills posted upside down. We can't read them, but maybe, if we were only a little bit wiser, we could make out something of their meaning, even if they be posted upside down. But by-and-bye they'll be turned right, and then we shall read them straight off from end to end."

"God'll learn us to read then," said Tom, with a quiet smile.

"To be sure," answered Nat; "why, I'd give a pound down now to know how to teach Suey her A B C. Our text last Sunday morning was, 'And they shall all be taught of God.'[1] Of course He has chosen to do it Himself, just as I'd be heart glad to teach Suey. Ah! I shan't be stupid and ignorant up yonder, Tom; and thee'll be no more sickly and starved; we'll learn of God, lad, thee and me, and the bills won't be upside down there."

"Nat," said Tom, after a pause, "I hanker so much after Phil, as never was. But father watches me, and I'm afeared to go to the school. I gave one of the boys an apple for him, with my love, yesterday; but I've not seen him this six weeks."

"Well," said Nat, sighing, "it's hard upon thee, Tom. But he's safe there; and who knows? some day thy father may be a good man. Maybe, if we could make out that bill of thine that's posted upside down, it says somewhere near the beginning, or in the middle, or at the end, 'Here Tom's father turned good,' or something of that sort; I can't put it into printed words. That 'ud be rare and happy, wouldn't it, Tom?"

"Ay," said Tom, with tears in his eyes; "that 'ud pay for all."

He sat silent and motionless for some minutes, seeing nothing of the crowd passing before him, while he fancied the happiness of having a good man for his father. He felt more comforted and strengthened by Nat's homely words than if he had been feasted at a plentiful table; and now, as the Infirmary clock struck the hour of two, he shook hands with Nat, and kissed little Suey, and hurried away to the market to fill his basket with cockles, for the tea-tables of the people living in the back streets about Ardwick.

---

1 John 6:45.

Chapter 15

"MY FATHER IS WITH ME"

The hope that some day or other his father's heart would be changed as his had been helped Tom much to endure the discomforts and miseries of his lot. The faint hungry grudging with which he had watched his father at his tasty meals no longer beset him; and his impatient chafing at the relationship which bound him to such a man passed into a grave pity and sorrow. He ceased to appeal to his heavenly Father against his earthly parent, but instead, he prayed for him with earnest and persevering supplication. He called him father now without any inward rebellion; and as far as it was possible he tried to obey and honor him. There were many things which Tom was obliged to see and do altogether at variance with the new feelings and desires of his heart, but which he felt bound to do because his father bade him. One of these was giving up his attendance at the night-school; and indeed he was generally too weary now of an evening to take the long walk from his present home to the school which he had been accustomed to attend. Only on the Sunday, a day which he considered as belonging altogether to his Father in heaven, he resisted; and neither threat nor persuasion could move him to break the laws, which he found laid down for keeping the Sabbath holy.

One evening after his work was done, he was spelling out a chapter in his Bible, which by this time was getting well worn, while his father was sitting in front of the fire, smoking his pipe, when Haslam bade him read out aloud, and not mutter the words in a half whisper. The verses he had just come to were these, and Tom read them in a slow and deliberate voice: "What man is there of you, whom if his son ask bread, will he give him a stone? Or if he ask a fish, will he give him a serpent? If ye then, being evil, know how to give good gifts to your children, how much more shall your Father which is in heaven give good things to them that ask Him."[1]

"What's the meaning of it?" asked Haslam, with a sneer upon his lips.

"I'm not sure," answered Tom timidly; "it seems as if it meant that God is more ready to give us good things than folks' fathers are sometimes. It says, 'How much more shall your Father which is in heaven give good things to them that ask Him.'"

"And who is thy Father in heaven?" asked Haslam.

"God," answered Tom.

"A fine Father!" continued Haslam; "and thou'rt a nice one to call God Father! Does He know thou'rt ragged and clemmed? Why, I serve the devil, and he's a better master. Which is best off, thee or me?"

"Me," answered Tom, steadily.

"Thee!" sneered Haslam; "how dost make that out?"

"I'm ragged and clemmed," said Tom, "but I'm happy, and nobody can make or meddle with my happiness. Thee couldn't never make me unhappy, father. Some day or other, as soon as God sees as it's the right time, I shall be better off, and I've only got to wait. But if thee waits, it's only for judgment, and sorrow, and anger, when God sees that it's time to punish thee. Oh,

1 Matthew 7:9–11.

father, I wish thee only believed what I believe!"

"What's that?" asked Haslam, filling his pipe again, and crushing the coals in the grate with his heavy boot.

"I can't rightly put it into words," answered Tom, earnestly, "but it's somehow in this way. Before I cared anything about God, or knew aught about Him, He was loving me all the time, and He sent Mr. Hope, and Mr. Banner, and Nat Pendlebury, to teach me that the Lord Jesus Christ came into the world to be my Savior; and He is my brother, just as I'm Phil's brother; and if I'd only believe in Him, and trust in Him, then God would be my Father, and I should become His son. Jesus loved us all so well that He died for us, just as I would die for little Phil; and now He is gone back to heaven to make our home there ready for us. I've only got to wait a little while, and then He'll take me home. Father, if thee'd only believe in Jesus, then God 'ud be thy Father."

"I want no father," said Haslam, with an oath; "I can fend for myself; and I'll bide the judgment thee talks of. But I want my boy Phil, and him I'll have. Where's he gone to, I ask thee? If thee keeps the secret from me any longer, I'll half kill thee."

There was an evil look in his father's eye, which made Tom quail for a moment; but his courage came back quickly.

"I'm not scared by thee," he said, his eye kindling, and his face brightening; "maybe thee thinks that the room is empty, and there's nobody to stand betwixt us. But God is here, and He sees everything that we do, and hears everything we say; and He can keep me safe. Ay, and He will keep me safe; or if it is His will that thee should kill me outright, why then He'll take me home to Him and the Lord Jesus, and I shall see His face, and stand among the angels. God is in the room, father."

Tom's bright keen eyes looked as if he could see more than his father saw, and Haslam glanced round with a fear and dread which had never possessed him before. He dropped down into his chair, from which he had started in his fury, and tried to whistle a merry tune, but the notes were quivering, and he took up his pipe again, and put it between his lips.

"Didst ever ask God for those good things He says He'll give thee?" he asked, after a long silence.

"Ay," answered Tom, quietly.

"Didst ever get them?" he asked, jeeringly.

"Ay, surely," said Tom; "before I knew He was my Father, I used to ask Him for clothes, and food, and money, and He gave them to me. I'd two good suits of clothes, as decent as I could wish; and I'd plenty to eat; and I'd seven pounds four shillings in the Savings Bank. Thee'd call them good things, I reckon?"

Haslam nodded his head as much as to say, "Yes."

"But of late," continued Tom, turning his eyes in a dreamy way to the fire, and speaking as if to himself, "ever since I knew He was my Father like, it seems as if I could ask for nothing but what's in the prayer, 'Our Father,' I used to count those things as wages for being good, and I thought God was like a master, and was paying me my wage. But now it's all different. He's my Father, and I don't want anything besides what He thinks best for me. As soon as it's time He'll give me food and clothes. There used to come strange thoughts into my head when I was starving in Liverpool. I didn't know what they meant then, but I do now. If He thought it best for me to lie down in the streets and die, I'd not be afeared but what He'd take me right up to heaven."

"Then what does thee ask thy Father for?" said Haslam, in his scoffing voice.

"I say 'Our Father,'" answered Tom, in the same dreamy way; and he murmured to himself, in a low half-whisper, all the prayer, asking for the Father's name to be hallowed, and the Father's kingdom to come, and the Father's will to be done;

then for himself only the daily bread, the forgiveness of sins, and the deliverance from temptation and evil. Haslam did not speak again, but as soon as he had smoked out his pipe he pushed back his chair, calling his son a canting hypocrite, and then started off on his mysterious nightly business.

Tom's room was untenanted now except by himself, but it was neither empty nor lonely. A poor, dirty, scantily furnished room it was, with patches of mildewed plaster on the walls, and with many footprints upon the bare floor. The smouldering fire scarcely lit it up, and it was, perhaps, better in the dimness than in a brighter light. From the room below, which was occupied by a large family, there came the sounds of rude laughter and wrangling. But Tom, bending over the fire, with his eyes still peering into its dull embers, saw and heard nothing of all his outer life. He could not have put his thoughts into words, but, as he had said, strange thoughts and fancies passed through his brain. Once he had been filled with dismay at the thought that God saw him always, and that had been his chief idea about God; it was the one truth concerning Him which had taken the strongest hold of his mind. Like the poor runaway slave Hagar, whom the angel of the Lord found in the wilderness, he called the name of the Lord who spake unto him, "Thou God seest me!"[1] Once, as you remember, this had been a source of terror and torment to him, and, if it had been possible, he would have endeavored to escape from the eye of God. But ever since he had known God by the name of Father, the thought of His perpetual presence had turned all his life into a solemn gladness and service. In the diligent reading of his thumb-worn Bible, he had come across this saying of the Savior, "Ye shall leave Me alone, and yet I am not alone, because the Father is with Me."[2] Tom

1 Genesis 16:13.
2 John 16:32.

thought he might say the same words; and often, at such times as this in the dusky room, or when he was sheltering from the spring showers under some archway, or resting his weary frame upon the steps of an empty house, this verse came into his heart with a sweetness and strength such as nothing else could give, and turning away his sad thoughts from his wicked father, and his failing strength, and his sore poverty, he would say to himself, "Yet I am not alone, because my Father is with me."

Chapter 16

LITTLE PHIL

The great annual holiday of the Lancashire people is Whitsun-week, when every man, woman, and child throughout the cotton manufacturing districts, regards it as a long-established right that some treat or other should be provided for him. Whit-Sunday fell late that year, but there was a pleasant surprise in store for Tom, for early in the morning Joey Pendlebury made his appearance with a bundle under his arm, upon which was written in Banner's well-known hand, "For Thomas Haslam with R. Banner's best wishes." It contained a new suit of fustian clothes, strong and serviceable, and a pair of clogs, such as Tom had not worn since his father had pawned the set of clothes which he had left behind him in his wretched flight to Liverpool. Tom sat down and cried for joy, and then made haste to dress himself in time to go to the church which Banner attended. Banner was standing before the church door in his uniform, until the congregation had assembled, and Tom grasped his hand and looked up into his face, but he was quite unable to speak a word. As for Banner, he had to loosen his stiff stock and clear his throat before he could bid him to go in and sit down in the first seat he came to in the gallery, which was the one the policeman occupied when his duty was over. It was near the organ, and Tom trembled as the deep booming tones resounded through the church, and seemed to come back again upon his ear; but it was a thrill of delight, not the trembling of fear; and in a little while his voice, faint but clear, joined in the chant and the hymn, and he felt overpoweringly happy.

But there was still another pleasure in store for him, the fore-taste of an undreamed-of delight. As they came out of church Banner gave him a ticket to go with Phil's school to Alderley, a place about twenty miles from Manchester, upon the following Thursday. The master of the school had given his permission for Tom to accompany them, and they were to start at half-past five o'clock in the morning, and spend the whole livelong day out in the country. Tom looked upon the ticket with a feeling almost of reverence, and he felt as if he should not be able to close his eyes at night for thinking of the joy that was to come.

There was a great enjoyment on the morning of Whit-Monday. All the Sunday-school teachers and scholars belonging to the churches in Manchester and Salford were accustomed to form processions from their various schools, and march with music and banners through the streets till they all met in St. Ann's Square, near the center of the city, and from thence, in one monster procession, to thread their way through a great crowd of spectators to the cathedral, where, once in the year, they all joined in public prayer to God. Tom was up at dawn in the morning, but the city was awake before him, and the sun, when it broke through the clouds that hung about it, shone down upon the busy streets, already filled with a joyous stir and tumult. By-and-bye, as the morning wore on, might be heard the distant sound of music in every quarter, but all tending to one center; and up from the side streets there came one after another long files of children gaily dressed, with flags herald-ing their way, and their feet marching in time to their bands of musicians. Tom had half hoped to hide himself in some corner in St. Ann's Square, but two ranks of policemen stretched across it from side to side, standing back to back and shoulder to shoulder, and at the word of command each rank marched forward, sweeping the square of all the bystanders, and driving them all into the side streets, so as to secure room for the gathering crowds of Sunday-schools. Tom was swept away with the rest, so he ran as quickly as he could to gain a good place on the road to the cathedral, where the whole of the procession must pass before his eyes; for it was little Phil he longed and hungered to see, as he marched along with his companions, the inmates of the school at Ardwick.

It was a good place under the cathedral walls which Tom managed to secure before the thickest of the throng gathered; for it would seem as if all the population of Manchester had turned out to see the children's procession. At last it began to file past through the middle of the crowd, along a path kept clear by the police force; and one school after another went by, closely regarded by Tom. But by-and-bye there could be heard in the distance a cheer and hurrah running along the throng, and coming nearer and nearer, such as had not greeted any of the other schools. It was the Ardwick Ragged School array, with its good band of music played by the boys themselves; and all the people shouted at the sight of these children, who had been saved from the vice, and misery, and ignorance of the streets. Tom's eyes were very dim, but his heart beat triumphantly; and he gazed through the mist of his tears for little Phil's fair hair and beautiful face. He saw him at last, and then he tossed his cap up into the air, and shouted as loudly as he could amid the din and clamor, "Hallo, Phil! little Phil!"

"So yon is little Phil!" said a voice in his ear, which made the glad throbbing of his heart stand still and the flush to die out of his face. It was his father's voice behind him, and he was gazing eagerly at the boys of the Ragged School, just as Phil, who was one of the youngest and last, caught sight of Tom, and beckoned gaily to him. Before Tom could speak, his father had pushed a way among the crowd, and was lost to his sight; but little Phil was turning round to look back upon him with his bright face. But for Tom, all the glory of the day and the brightness of the spectacle were faded, and a great dread of Phil's future had fallen upon him. If his father should persist in claiming him, and insist upon removing him from the school, what a terrible change it would make in the young child's life! He had borne wretchedness and privation, and the sights and sounds of evil for himself, but he felt as if he could never bear them for Phil. He shuddered to think of him hearing the wicked language he heard, and seeing the wickedness he was forced to see. Tom had never told what he suffered, even to Nat Pendlebury and Alice; and much less to Banner would he have betrayed the vices of his father. But if little Phil were to be brought into close home-fellowship with them—why, he had far rather a thousand times follow little Phil's coffin to some quiet grave.

The music was still playing and the streamers flying, but Tom gave no heed to either. He gave up his good place to a boy who had been long jostling him, and wended his way homewards, half fearing and half hoping to meet his father. But Haslam was not there, and Tom took his basket, and with a very sad heart went off to the market for supplies. His customers must be provided with food, however heavy his spirit was, and so he toiled along his customary route until evening. Haslam was still absent when he reached home, and, in spite of his dejection, Tom soon fell into a weary slumber, which was not broken by his father's return during the night.

But before Tom could set out again for another day's work,

he felt that he must find out his father's purposes with regard to little Phil. It did not seem a favorable moment for speaking, for his father had been drinking heavily overnight, and now was suffering from the effects of it. But he could not go away uncertain whether or no he should see Phil in their close and dirty lodging room when he returned at night.

"Father," he said, "father, thee sees how well off little Phil is! He's got good clothes, and good food, and good learning, and all for nothing! Thee will let him be at his school, and not go making work about him? He'll cost thee a sight of money if he comes out."

"I'll have him out!" cried Haslam, "I'll have him out, and make him of use to me, for thou'rt worth nothing to me. Who's so much right to the lad as his own father? The chaplain 'ud tell the police I'm a changed man, and quite fit to train up my own child. I can teach him to sing psalms and say prayers as well as any of them. I must have the training of little Phil. A trim, bright little fellow as I ever set eyes on! I'll make a man of him! Who was it put him into that school, I want to know?"

"Mr. Worthington!" answered Tom, with a faint hope of influencing his father. "It's Worthington's mill where Mr. Pendlebury is the night-watchman."

"Worthington!" answered Haslam, fiercely; "why, it's him that got me sent to jail for ten years; and it was his wife's brother—Hope, his name is—that set the judge and jury dead against me, when I might have got off but for him. It 'ud spite them a little to take Phil from the school, though that's not all the revenge I'll have. Thee hast settled my mind for me, lad."

"Oh, father!" cried Tom, falling down on his knees, "just hearken to me for once. Don't thee bring little Phil here! Don't learn him to swear, and steal, and drink! Leave him where he is, and I'll do almost anything to please thee. I'd almost be a thief again for little Phil to have a chance of growing up good."

"Get up, blockhead!" said Haslam, "and be off with thee. Phil's my son, and I'll have him. I suppose if nobody had taken a fancy to him, he'd have been thrown on my hands to keep. They'd make no work about taking him out of a workhouse; and I'll have him out of the school. He'll be of more use to me than thee; for thou hast a hang-dog, jail-bird look about thee that 'ud frighten folks."

"Then," said Tom, with a white but resolute face, "as sure as ever thee brings Phil into this place, I'll tell Mr. Banner all I know about thee. I'll tell him that thou'rt out all night, and that thou art not the changed man thee boasts of. He'll believe me; and maybe he can get the justices to say thou'rt not fit to have the care of little Phil. I don't want to do it, father; but as sure as ever I see little Phil in this room, I'll go straight off to Mr. Banner."

There was a baffled and vicious expression upon Haslam's face, but he was silent for a while, and when he spoke it was in a quiet and conciliatory manner. He would let Phil be for a while, he said; but he must go and see him, and let him know his father; for maybe he was not happy in the school, and then Tom would not object to having him out. There floated before Tom's mind a vision of a quiet home with a good man for his father, and little Phil living with them, and growing up before his eyes into a good and clever man. But it was a dream only, and with a sigh of mingled regret and thankfulness he bade his father good-morning, and went out with a heart once more at rest.

Chapter 17

A DAY AT ALDERLEY

t was one of the brightest of mornings, as if the sun himself were rejoicing in the "Whit-week" holiday, when Tom, with the boys and girls of the Ardwick School, marched in procession to the station at Longsight, where a train was appointed to meet them, and to take them down to Alderley. There were more schools and more excursion trains bound for the same place, and others; and there reigned everywhere a holiday feeling, which might have been brought by the fresh air and the sunshine. Phil held Tom's hand, and looked radiant with happiness, while from Tom's face the cloud of habitual care and thought passed away, and a bright but quiet smile took its place. They had not to wait long before they were fairly on their way, passing through meadows and cornfields, where the blades of corn were still young and green; fields such as Tom had never seen before, for last Whit-week his love of saving money had been too strong to permit him to take a day from his business, and to spend a few shillings upon pleasure. By half-past six o'clock in the morning, as the country people were fetching in their cows to be milked from the pastures, and while there was all the cool freshness of the day, they reached Alderley; and then, with their own brass band playing gaily, they

marched through the village to a farm-house where a breakfast of bread-and-milk was provided for them. It was all a grave
and solemn festival to Tom, filled to the brim with satisfaction,
because Phil, with his beautiful face, was marching at his side;
and a hundred times in his inmost heart, pressing Phil's hand
with a tighter grasp, he thanked God that his father would not
dare to take him away from the school.

As soon as breakfast was over, they were free to go wherever they liked, provided that they returned at noon for their
dinner. Then the enjoyment increased and deepened. All the
Pendleburys had come down by another train, and they and
Tom and Phil had agreed to be a complete party of themselves.
They rambled leisurely along shady lanes, where the trees on
each side threw upon their path alternate lights and shadows,
dancing with a restless motion, so full of life that Tom and Alice
said they hardly liked to set their feet upon the ground for fear of
hurting them; but the little ones chased the sunbeams and shadows with shouts of merriment, and danced upon them in their
glee. The hedgerows seemed laden here and there with snow
from the profusion of hawthorn blossoms, and every breath of
the soft wind scattered their tiny flakes upon the grassy banks
beneath. And what a wind it was! No more like the keen east
winds of March, which had stung Tom in his thin clothing,
than a dreary day in November is like a day of sunny June.
It came whispering and rustling very softly through the young
leaves, which had never yet been dusty and hot with summer
dryness, and bending down gently the tall blades of grass, which
were ripening fast for the hay-harvest, and kissing away the deli-
cate bloom from the fruit-trees. It brought with it, too, such
sweet scents of wild flowers, of bluebells and cowslips, and hon-
eysuckle, which just floated about them without making the
air too heavy with their perfume. It played lightly with Alice's

ribbons, and stirred Phil's curls, and breathed coolly upon Tom's temples, which ached so often with the weight of his basket. It seemed difficult to remember the smoke and the dense atmosphere of the city; and to Tom it was almost a delicious pain to breathe the fresh, sweet, pure air of the country. He drank it in as one parched with thirst in a burning desert would drink at a spring of cold water.

They came at last to a wood, where trees of great beauty had been growing for many years, carefully tendered and fostered, yet left to grow luxuriantly and healthily according to their own nature. Here the shadows were thicker, for overhead the branches formed a canopy, which sheltered them well from the growing heat of the morning sun; while under foot, instead of the hard high-road, there was smooth green turf, strewed with daisies and moss, into which their feet sank softly and soundlessly. Every now and then they came to dingles, in whose hollows the tall ferns grew, and down whose sloping sides the children rolled themselves with shrieks of laughter. Sometimes there lay before them solemn glades, stretching far away, like the long aisles of some grand cathedral, with boughs arching and mingling high up above their heads, as if some taller and greater beings than themselves were wont to walk to and fro there, or form processions with banners and streamers which rose far aloft. The little ones ran down these grassy aisles, shouting to the squirrels in the trees, and to the birds which flew leisurely above the topmost branches; but Nat and Alice walked along almost in silence, and Tom sighed often, from a profound and inexpressible delight.

They sat down after a while, not to rest, there was no feeling of fatigue in them, but for the slower and fuller enjoyment of their pleasure. The trees were more open in the spot they had chosen, and the blue sky, flecked all over with tiny cloudlets, and streaked here and there with a fine feathery film, that only

THE DAY AT ALDERLY.

made the sky behind it look a deeper blue, stretched above the green summits of the oaks and elms. I said they felt no fatigue, but Tom was weary—if a feeling of delicious languor and leisure can be called weariness. He lay down upon the velvet turf, with his face upturned to the sky, and his eyes opening and closing as the flitting shadows of the leaves above him played upon his eyelids. He scarcely knew whether he was awake or dreaming; but such a dream had never visited him before. It was very quiet; for very soon Nat and the children rambled off in search of some new enchantment, and only Alice and Phil remained behind; for somehow neither Alice nor Phil could bear to leave Tom's side that day. There was the pleasant rustling of leaves to be heard, and the soft far-off call of the cuckoo, and now and then a distant sound of laughter; but there was no harsh shrill din and tumult of busy toiling life—no rattling of wheels or whirl of machinery; and Tom lay there, with Phil's hand resting on his head, and Alice sitting where he could see her, if he opened his eyelids by a hair's-breadth. But whether he was awake or dreaming he could not tell.

"Alice," he said at last, in a low tone, lest he should awake and find it was a dream, "Alice, dost thee think heaven'll be like this?"

"Ay, maybe," she answered, softly; "only we shall see God, and we shall hear the angels playing on their harps, and it'll be sweeter music than the birds singing; and maybe wherever we look we shall see the face of God smiling at us for ever and ever. Heaven'll be far better than this, Tom."

Tom lay still again for a little while, gazing up steadfastly into the blue sky, so very far and so very high above his head, and as he looked a deep and tender smile spread itself over his features, so that Alice and Phil, seeing it, wondered at the strange beauty which changed his careworn and famished features, and Phil, stooping down, kissed Tom's wrinkled forehead.

"Ah!" said Tom, still in the same low voice, "He is smiling at us now. God smiles at us. I never saw my father smile at me, never! But God loves us dearly. I don't mind now about going back to Manchester. A while since I was hankering in myself to stay here always, and never go back to the work and the noise— it tires me, and makes my head ache, and it's so quiet here, and good. But now, if God'll only smile at me, I'd go and live in a jail, or a workhouse, and wait His time to take me out of them. I'm content now."

"But thee'd choose to live out here in the country?" said Alice.

"Ay," murmured Tom, "if He chose it. But I don't care so much now; He'll choose what is best for me. Heaven'll be something like this, Alice. I don't know anything about it: I don't know where the wind comes from, or what makes the sun shine, and the trees grow, and the little flowers peep up among the grass—only that it is God's work. I don't know what God calls them all, only He made them, and they are all beautiful—oh, how beautiful they are! And it'll be the same in heaven. I shan't know anything when I get there, only that God made them all, and knows the name of every angel. And He'll know my name, and I shall hear Him call me by it; and I shall speak back to Him, and call Him Father."

"Tom," said Alice, in a tone half frightened, "thee loves God better than I do."

"No, no!" answered Tom, earnestly, with the same quiet and loving smile upon his face; "thee has loved Him longer than me, and thee was never so wicked as I have been. Thee went to Sunday-school when thou wert a very little girl; and thee never swore, or stole, or hardly told a lie all thy life. God has forgiven me more sins than thee. But I think He loves us all alike—everybody who believes in the Lord Jesus. Thy father does not love one more than another; and it's the same with God. Only it's thee that has served Him and loved Him the longest. And I must make up for the lost time, thee knows, as well as I can. I ought to love Him more nor thee, for I was a thief, and my father was a thief."

"Dost think of God often?" asked Alice, quietly.

"He's always there," said Tom, drawing little Phil's hand upon his breast, and pressing it against his heart. "He's always speaking to me now; and sometimes I forget that I'm in the street, and I go along seeing nothing, and hearing nothing. Eh, Alice, if thee had nothing else in the world, nothing but God, thee couldn't help but think of Him often. I don't know much about Him, but every day I seem to learn more. The thoughts come into my head of themselves: I don't know where from. It isn't only when I'm reading my Bible, or saying my prayers, but wherever I go there seems to be a voice teaching me about Him. What can it be, Alice?"

"It must be God's Holy Spirit," answered Alice, with a thoughtful and downcast face. "Jesus said, 'I will pray the Father, and He shall give you another Comforter, that He may abide with you for ever; even the Spirit of Truth, whom the world cannot receive, because it seeth Him not, neither knoweth Him; but ye know Him, because He dwelleth with you, and shall be in you.'"[1]

"Ay," cried Tom, joyously; "then Jesus has prayed the Father to give me the Comforter! I understand now. And He dwells with me, and is in me; so the thoughts come from Him. And He is with thee, Alice, and with thy father."

"Not always," said Alice, with tears in her eyes; "the Bible says we can grieve the Spirit; and very often I grieve Him, and then He leaves me for a little while. Oh, Tom, I wish I loved God as well as thee!"

1 John 14:16–17.

"I think thee does," answered Tom, tenderly. "It's like a new thing to me, thee knows. I only love God by thinking how He loves me. I can't do anything to serve Him worth speaking of, only all day long I mind how He loves me, so I cannot help loving Him back again. Ay, heaven'll be something like this. I shan't know anything about it, only God knows all, and He'll know me."

They sank into silence again, listening to the songs of the birds, and looking at the trees about them. It was true what Tom had said: they did not know what birds were singing, nor what were the names of the trees and flowers around them; but God had made them all, and they were all good. It was a scene of strange delight and peace, and to Tom's weary frame and spirit a place of delicious rest. He did not care to stir, or to ramble about in search of fresh pleasures. When he had sunk down in pleasant weariness, there he stayed, with little Phil and Alice still lingering faithfully beside him, until it was time to return to the farm.

When evening came, and Tom, after bidding farewell to the Pendleburys, at the corner of Pilgrim Street, turned his tired feet towards the close and squalid court where his home was, and where his father lived, he sang softly to himself, in a sweet but feeble voice, two verses of the hymn which had been sung by all the children of Ardwick School before leaving Alderley. They were these:

> "For ever with the Lord!
>   Amen, so let it be!
> Life from the dead is in that word,
>   'Tis immortality.
>
> Here in the body pent,
>   Absent from Him I roam;
> Yet nightly pitch my moving tent
>   A day's march nearer home!"

Chapter 18

FAIR APPEARANCES

As soon as the revelry and drunkenness of Whit-week were over, Haslam paid his threatened visit to the school on Ardwick Green, and demanded, in a civil but resolute manner, to see his son. He knew that he had the power to withdraw him from the school, as he was not there, like many of the boys, under an order from the magistrates; but it was not his wish to provoke Tom to fulfil his threats, or to call upon himself the unpleasant notice of Banner and the police. To the master of the school he presented himself in the character of a decent mechanic who had long since, under prison discipline, repented of his former evil course, and was anxious to live honestly and laboriously for the future. Towards little Phil, Haslam was so gentle and affectionate that he easily won the child's simple heart, and Phil clung fondly to him when it was time for him to leave. It appeared quite a reasonable thing to the master that Haslam should wish his boy to spend his holidays at his own home, instead of in Pilgrim Street; and Banner himself, when he heard it spoken of, could not raise any sufficient objection, though a vague misgiving occasionally crossed his mind that Haslam was not quite what he should be.

I do not know whether to call Phil's visits home a pain or

a pleasure to Tom. It was very pleasant to see little Phil often again, and listen to all the stories he had to tell about his school, and see what rapid progress he was making in his reading and writing, for he had shot far ahead of Tom, and now could teach him many things of which he was ignorant. But there was a deep pain lurking behind the pleasure, for his father was gaining great influence over the child by indulging and flattering him; and by-and-bye little Phil began to show a good share of self-conceit and obstinacy. More than this, it was soon plain that he liked to taste the intoxicating liquors in which Haslam indulged, and he listened with boyish interest to Haslam's boasts and vaunts about his former life, which had been full of adventure and narrow escapes from the just punishment of his crimes. Tom was seldom at home all the time of Phil's visits, for his work kept him out till a late hour in the evening; but he could see sorrowfully the change that was creeping over his young brother, and more than once, in the keen agony and dread of his spirit, he prayed to the heavenly Father to take little Phil away out of the world into the safety and purity of heaven.

It was one evening that Phil was spending with his father and Tom, and as it so happened he was reading aloud a chapter in the Bible to show them how well he could do it, when there came a loud knock at the door, and when Tom hastened to open it there stood Mrs. Worthington and Nat Pendlebury, accompanied by a strange gentleman. The scene before these three visitors wore a good and pleasing aspect. There sat Haslam with little Phil standing at his knee, and before them on the small table lay an open Bible; and though the room was squalid and dirty, Mrs. Worthington remembered immediately that there was no woman belonging to it to keep it clean and comfortable. Tom saw an expression of fear and hatred come over his father's face as he rose slowly from his chair, as if scarcely knowing what to do or say, but the gentleman who accompanied Mrs. Worthington approached him with an outstretched hand.

"Shake hands with me," said he, in a friendly tone; "I have heard good news of you, Haslam, and I am come to say let bygones be bygones. You have not forgotten Mr. Ross, have you?"

"The chaplain at the jail, sir? oh, no!" answered Haslam.

"I saw him yesterday," continued the gentleman. "He dined with my wife and me at Knutsford. He said nothing but good of you, Haslam; and we were both heartily glad to hear it. We brought Pendlebury with us to find out your lodgings, and he says the same of you. Are you in any regular work yet, my man?"

"No, sir," replied Haslam, humbly; "everything goes against me. There's not many masters 'ud take a ticket-of-leave man, and I wouldn't go into any master's service without telling him first."

"Quite right, my good fellow," said Mr. Worthington; "there's nothing like being straightforward and open. I know all about you, Haslam, and I say, let there be no old grudge between us, but let bygones be bygones. You have a fine little lad there, and Mrs. Worthington has taken a great fancy for him; we will see to him getting on in life. Banner speaks well of Tom, too. But you must find it hard to get a living by doing odd jobs. You need regular work and wages to make you comfortable."

"Ay, sir," answered Haslam, "for Tom's earnings are small, but we make them serve. We're content with little to eat, and the rent isn't much. I can't ask the lady to sit down in a poor place like this. I was a respectable man once, sir, and well to do."

"Well, well," said Mr. Worthington, "it may be so again, Haslam. I'll tell you our errand here tonight. There's a vacancy for a carpenter in my mill, with constant employment. It is the sort of work you were once accustomed to. Do you think you could undertake the place now?"

"Could I?" said Haslam, with a strange gleam in his eyes; "ay, could I! And a hundred thanks to you, sir, for offering to try me again at the old mill, where I worked when I was a boy. You'll never forget it; you'll never forget doing me a kindness. It was a kindness of you sending me to jail; it'll be nine years ago this next assizes, and I've never forgotten it. I should never have been the man I am but for you and Mr. Hope."

"And the good chaplain," added Mrs. Worthington. "But we are to forget the bad old times, Haslam, and only remember these better days. Phil there is getting a good scholar—one of the best boys in the school at Ardwick, so the master tells me."

"Ay, ma'am," answered Haslam; "he's learning well, is Phil; but I feel it hard to be parted from one of my boys, and some of the lads at the school are very bad company for him. He's been telling me things about them that make me uneasy, and I've found many faults in Phil which are a sore grief to me. I'd take him home if I could afford it, and, train the little lad myself. There's nobody can feel like a father, though I'm but a poor sort of father, I know. Why, ma'am, most of the boys there are sent by order of the magistrates. It's a kind of jail for wicked boys, and my little Phil isn't a bad child though it's me that says so, and I don't like him to keep company with them. They can't have a master always with them, and if it wouldn't offend you, I'd like to take him out. Sometimes I think I ought, whether or no."

"I'm sorry to hear this about the school," said Mrs. Worthington, with a grave face; "but you must not do it rashly, Haslam. It's quite natural for you to be anxious, but you could not bring little Phil here. When you are in better circumstances come and talk with me about it, and I'll make some inquiries about the school. We must say good-bye now."

"I'll light you down the stairs, ma'am," said Haslam, taking the candle in his hand, and going down the steep and crooked staircase before his visitors. He returned with a strange bad smile and a look of triumph on his face; but he said nothing, and Tom could not guess what he was thinking about. Soon afterwards it was time for Phil to go back to school, and Haslam said he would walk up to Ardwick Green with him, as Tom was too wearied with his day's work, and he did not come in again until long after Tom had fallen into a heavy and feverish slumber upon his hard bed.

The next week Haslam entered upon his new and regular employment at Worthington's mill. The wages were good, and he was able to indulge himself more constantly in dainty things to eat and drink; but he had less liberty, and he was cut off from his nightly rambles, wherever they might have been. Tom did not expect him to keep the place long, but still he went on steadily from week to week, very much to Tom's surprise and satisfaction. There was, moreover, greater thought and reflection evidently at work in his mind. At night, after his supper was finished, he would sit still and think, with his head sunk upon his breast, and his eyelids closed; and now and then his lips would move, as if his thoughts were about to shape themselves into audible words. There were other good signs of a change, which Tom saw with great thankfulness. He made friends with Nat Pendlebury, and would sometimes stay with him for an hour after the other hands had left the mill, fondling and playing with his dog, and talking about Alice and the little ones at home. Nat's guileless heart rejoiced greatly over him, and he began to feel sure that they had reached that place in the bill of Tom's life where it was set down, "Here Tom's father turned good."

Both Mr. Worthington and Banner heard the good report of Haslam with much satisfaction, and the latter immediately proposed to Tom to set him up in his former mode of doing business, only with a better and smarter donkey-cart. The time was come when it was necessary that Tom should be relieved from the heavy weight of his basket, for though he never complained of it, he felt his strength failing more and more every day; yet he hesitated a long while before he would accept Banner's hearty offer, and it was only when he said he would rather the trial was made and failed, than not undertaken at all, that Tom at last consented. Even Haslam took an interest in the new cart, and did a few carpentering jobs at it to fit it up better for Tom's use; and once again the boy found himself driving in a business-like way from the market to the streets where his customers dwelt. The long and bitter trial seemed past. His father had apparently entered fully upon a changed and reformed life, and he himself had been permitted to take up again the position which he had forfeited by his short-sighted sin. But it was not now as in the former days. No more had the love of money power to sway one thought of Tom's heart; he had set his affections firmly upon things above, and as the coins began to chink again in his money-bag, they had little music for him, except as they reminded him to thank the Father, from whom cometh every good gift and every perfect gift.

But still Haslam was in no hurry to change his cheap lodgings for some more decent and more expensive. He was saving his money, he said, to make a thorough change, and to get a home good enough to bring little Phil to. Tom did not dread this as much as he had once done, and he was willing enough to give up his own earnings to increase the sum of his father's savings, which Haslam put by week after week in a strong box, cunningly concealed under the ceiling of their room; for, as he said, it would be of no use to deposit the money in the Savings Bank, when they would want it out so soon. Tom and Alice began to look out for a little house not far from Pilgrim Street, which would do for the new home, and be near enough for Alice to run in sometimes and put everything tidy. It was just possible that a neighboring house might be vacant in the course of a few weeks; but the tenants in Pilgrim Street were used to remain a long time, as it was a respectable and quiet little court, through which there was no thoroughfare. Still there was a hope, and in the meantime they could do nothing better than wait patiently, and look out for any vacancy in the immediate neighborhood.

Chapter 19

THE LOCKED DOOR

All the mill hands were leaving Worthington's mill at the usual hour one night, when Nat Pendlebury reached the gates to enter upon his duty as night-watchman. Two or three of the clerks were detained by business a little beyond six o'clock, but they also were soon gone, and Nat was left alone with Colin, his little watch-dog. There was a small office just within the gates, where a fire was left burning for him, with a table on the hearth, upon which he carefully deposited his supper, which he had brought in a basin, tied up in a blue and white check handkerchief. It was quite dark now by seven, for the shorter days after Michaelmas were come round again, and Nat lighted his lantern, and called his dog to make their customary round through the mill, before settling down for a quiet hour or two, until it was time to fire his gun at ten o'clock, and again make the round to see that everything was quite right. He mounted to the topmost story of the building, and descended slowly from floor to floor, passing through every part of the factory, where the ghostly machinery, only a short time ago so full of whirl and motion, now stood still, waiting, as it seemed, only for a word or a breath to start it off again on its restless labors. The dog ran in and out amongst the looms, as he had been trained to do, and once he gave a sharp sudden bark, which arrested Nat's steps for a moment, and made him turn his lantern about in every direction. But as soon as he whistled, Colin came up quietly and quickly enough, without any further sign of excitement; and Nat went on from room to room, until he came back to his own little office.

It was Nat's custom, as soon as he had made his first round, to kneel down and ask the protection of God for himself and the mill during the night, after which he had a vague but pleasant feeling of having angels about him, commissioned to take charge of him, and to keep him in all his ways. He could not read, but his mind was always active, as he could remember much of what Alice read to him before setting out on his night's work. As it would not do for a faithful watchman to be found sleeping, he employed himself in repeating aloud every passage of Scripture which he could recall, and in singing one after the other all the hymns he knew, an employment which carried him far on into the night; for now and then he was obliged to stop to rest himself, and to take breath. Whatever Nat did, he did with all his might, and singing was no languid exercise with him.

He was just pouring some coffee into a stone bottle, to warm up on the hob, ready for his supper at half-past ten, when there came a ring at the gate bell, which caused him to suspend his occupation with a feeling of surprise, and some little uneasiness. It was already after nine o'clock, and it was an unusual thing to have any visitor so late; but Nat did not linger to indulge in any guesses, but going briskly to the gateway, opened a small square trap-door, through which he could speak, or take a survey, without throwing open the great gates.

"It's only me, Mr. Pendlebury," said Tom's voice, "father's never come home yet, and I came along to ask if thee had seen aught of him tonight. He's not used to be so late."

"No, Tom," answered Nat, "I've seen nought of thy father today. The mill was pretty nigh loosed afore I came in. What makes thee anxious about father, Tom?"

"I don't know," said Tom; "father's been very steady of late, since he came to the mill. But, Mr. Pendlebury," and the boy's voice was lowered to a whisper, "there's a strange thing happened at our house. Thee knows father and I have been laying by our savings, and he said it was of no use putting it into the bank, because we shall want it soon to buy things for our new house, before Phil comes to live at home, and so we kept it in a place that only he and me knew of. But it's gone, the money is! There's the box all right enough, but the key was left in the lock, and the money is gone. Father has taken the money for something or other, and he is not come home tonight. It's nigh upon fifteen pounds, for he's been very saving of late. I don't know what ever to think!"

"He was gone," said Nat, "afore I got in, for I asked after him to show him a door that doesn't shut quite right, and one of the hands said that he were gone. Maybe thee will find him at home by now, Tom."

"Maybe I shall," replied Tom; "for little Phil has been to see us, and he stayed till eight o'clock, and then I went to the school with him, and I came round by here, instead of going back. Maybe father's at home by now."

"Sure to be," said Nat; "why, Tom, thou were dreaming to come here after him! Thee only gave him two hours' grace. He's at home, sure enough."

"It's very lonesome inside the mill at night," remarked Tom.

"Not for me," answered Nat. "I'm as lively as a bird all night, Tom—Colin and me. The dog knows my favorite hymns, and listens to me singing quite reasonable. Oh no! it's not lonesome at all."

"Well, good night, Mr. Pendlebury," said Tom.

"Good night, Tom," replied Nat.

Nat listened to the sound of Tom's wooden clogs clattering along the quiet street; for Worthington's mill was situated in a very quiet and lonely part of the city. An old mill it was, too, having been built by the present Mr. Worthington's grandfather; and it had been greatly enlarged and improved, though it yet bore an old-fashioned look, and the walls were grimy and black with the smoke of many years.

Nat turned into his room again for his lantern, and once more made a complete round of the premises. As the clocks of the city struck ten, at most of the mills a gun was discharged, to show that the watchman was on duty; and Nat fired his as soon as he heard the first sharp report in his neighborhood. It was a little after ten before he had completed his circuit, and by the time he came back to the office his coffee in the stone bottle was nearly boiling, and the basin of mashed potatoes and bacon beside it was well warmed through. Nat spread an old newspaper on the table, and placed his supper on it, after which he opened his large pocket knife, and was about to begin his meal, when Colin, after a low growl or two, sprang towards the door, and barked vehemently.

"What ails thee tonight, Colin?" asked Nat, getting up from his comfortable chair and opening the door, where he stood for a minute, holding the candle above his head, and peering into the darkness which lay beyond its feeble beams. Colin bounded out into the court, but he was pacified in an instant, and when Nat called, he came back again, and stretched himself once more on the hearth, which he beat softly with his tail, as he eyed Nat's movements with an air of lazy and perfect content. Nat sat down again, and went on with his supper, leaving a portion of it at the bottom of the basin for his dog, which was in a state of pleasurable excitement and commotion as soon as his master closed his clasp-knife and poured his coffee into a pint can.

"Colin, old fellow, there is thy share," said Nat, stooping to place the basin on the floor; but as he did so he fancied he heard a slight noise behind him, and turning his head round he saw that the door had been pushed ajar, and a hand was just taking the key out of the lock inside. His surprise held him only a moment, but before he could reach the door it was drawn to with a bang, and the key was hastily fitted into the lock, and turned, while Nat stood staring in amazement, and Colin, unmindful of his supper, gazed anxiously into his master's face. As soon as he recovered himself Nat rushed to the door; but his fancy had not deceived him; the lock was secured from the outside, and he was made a helpless prisoner.

For a few minutes Nat remained motionless, with his hand upon the latch, trying to realize his position. His room was a small office inside the factory, with the window only looking out upon the small square court about which the mill was built. He could see from it the windows of most of the rooms; but there was not the smallest chance of making himself heard into the street, which, of course, lay outside the buildings. The bell which summoned the mill hands to their work every morning at six o'clock, and by which he might have given an alarm, and brought a thousand people to his aid, hung just outside the door, and he could have reached it from the threshold, but with the door locked it might as well have been on the other side of the mill. He shook the lock again and again, but it was too secure and too strong to give way, and he quickly gave up his useless efforts. The window was a good height in the wall, but by standing on a chair he could see through it very well. For a minute he thought of trying to force his way through it; but at one time the room had been used as a counting-house,

NAT LOCKED IN.

and the casement was so strongly barred that Nat at once saw that the attempt would be impracticable, even if he met with no resistance from his unknown jailer outside. He put out his own light, and looked cautiously into the small court. Everything was perfectly quiet, and so dark that it was only after a few minutes he could make out the stiff straight outlines of the building, with the black line of the roof crossing the blackness of the sky, with only the faintest, most ghastly glimmer of pale light twinkling upon the glass panes of the many windows in the walls, which rose story after story up to the high roof. One pane in the barred casement of the office was made to open and Nat unfastened it with a cautious hand. There was not a sound to be heard, except the hum of city life, which rose and fell, sometimes louder and sometimes lower, telling of thousands of fellow-beings almost within hearing of his call; but within the mill there was no sign of the presence of a living person. Yet that there was somebody prowling about with an evil and malicious design Nat knew only too well, and suddenly there came into his mind the conversation he had held with Tom, not much more than an hour ago, through the little trap-door. Could it be possible that Haslam had concealed himself in the mill after the rest of the work people had gone away, for some wicked or revengeful purpose? He remembered Colin's sharp bark, so speedily silenced, when he was running in and out amongst the machinery; and his disquietude just before supper, so quickly pacified as soon as he had let him out into the court. Haslam had made friends with the dog, and accustomed him to be fondled by him, so that Colin would not continue to bark at him, when he discovered only a friend. But what could Haslam intend to do? Had he a gang outside who would rob the mill, and carry off the fabrics which were finished, and only needed to be sent to the packers? Or was there some worse design still in his mind, that he thus secreted himself in the buildings? Was it, moreover, really Haslam? He had seen only a hand, and there had been nothing in Haslam's manner to excite suspicion; yet Nat could not turn away his thoughts from Tom's father. He stood upon the chair peering out into the dark and silent court, unable to do anything, and waiting in helpless and anxious suspense for the next sign of the presence of his unknown jailer.

Chapter 20

THE FIRE AT THE MILL

N at Pendlebury kept his watch until his eyes began to ache, and his knees grow weary; but still there was nothing to be seen or heard, and he began to think that it was only a joke played upon him. At last he could hardly be sure whether his strained eyeballs did not deceive him, but here and there he thought he saw tiny sparks of light dance for a moment and then disappear. But they increased and strengthened, and instead of the deep darkness and the ghostly glimmer of the pale windows, there were flashes of red beams, and a ruddy tinge spreading within the inner rooms of the mill, which could not soon be seen from the streets without. It sparkled and brightened with a steady growth, and now there was no longer a question as to the evil design of the miscreant,[1] whoever he might be, that had been concealed in the mill. Once more Nat ran at the door, and set himself with all his strength to burst it open; but the lock, like the bars of the window, was too strongly made to yield to his vain attempts. There was no danger for himself, he knew; for long before the fire could reach his side of the buildings the alarm would have been given, and he would be rescued. But the work

1 Miscreant—an unprincipled or unscrupulous person.

of the incendiary[1] was being so skillfully done that the fire would have gained head long before it was discovered, and no efforts would avail to save the mill, and probably the buildings adjoining it. Now in the increasing light he saw once or twice the dark figure of a man passing and repassing the brightening windows; and after a few minutes, which seemed an age to Nat, he could see that he was making his way to the room where the raw cotton, soft as down, and inflammable as tinder, was kept. If that were fired the whole place was doomed. For another moment or two Nat was held in suspense, and then a strong clear flame was visible, and the first window was cracked by the heat. With a burst of beautiful and steady blaze the fire shot up above the roof of the building, and the clouds overhead grew red and lurid with its beams.

There was no longer silence in the quiet streets. Before the flame had burned many minutes, there was the sound of a gathering multitude, and the cry of "Fire! fire!" echoing from mouth to mouth. Then came the rattling of fire engines, and the thundering at the great gates, until they gave way with a crash. The first men who rushed into the court did not hear Nat's voice begging to be let out; but the door was opened at last by the hand of Banner himself, who had been one of the first policemen attracted by the blaze. In a few sentences Nat told him the story of his imprisonment, and pointed out the window at which he had last seen the incendiary. But by this time all the upper story of that side of the mill was in flames, and the casement to which Nat pointed fell in as they looked at it. No doubt the villain, whoever he was, had made good his escape, or might even now be mingling with the crowd, and looking on triumphantly at the mischief he had wrought. So tumultuous had been the rush of people into the court, that without difficulty he

1 Incendiary—Any person who sets fire to a building.

could have lost himself in the throng, and so passed by without exciting suspicion.

Nat and Banner were still looking up at the gap where the window had been not a minute before, when a white face, white from the ruddy flush upon every other face, was thrust between them, and they saw Tom standing there with a look of horror in his eyes. He could hardly utter the words with which his parched lips quivered, but with a strong effort he spoke to them at last.

"Father's in the mill!" he said, in a terrified voice. "I saw him at the window yonder only this moment. See there!"

They looked up as he pointed to one of the windows in the topmost story, and there looked down upon the crowd below Haslam's evil face, all lit up in the vivid brightness, until they could see with an awful distinctness his teeth clenched over his under lip, and his eyes glaring with terror. He was in the last room of the mill, and the other end, where there was the only outlet, was already in flames. For an instant neither of them could move or speak, but then Banner rushed to where the firemen were working the engines.

"There's a man in the mill!" he shouted, and immediately every face in the crowd was turned towards the window where Haslam stood, and the engines were set to play upon the flames in that story. Almost before one could think of it a ladder was brought; but the fire in the room underneath was already too strong for any one to venture near their intense fierceness, and it had to be set up at a little distance, while Haslam, in the extremity of his fear, saw nothing of the efforts made to save him. He ran from window to window shrieking for help, and every now and then trying to force his way through the flames towards the door, by which there was a bare chance of escape; unless someone had courage enough to make his way through the suffocating smoke, and the probability of an outbreak of fire from the story below, he must inevitably perish. But the peril was a great one, and even the firemen hesitated to enter into it.

"Let me go!" cried Tom, forcing his way to the foot of the ladder; "I'm his son, and he is my father. He is my father, I tell thee," he said to the firemen, who would have pushed him back, "and he doesn't love God."

What it was in the boy's white and solemn face, and in the voice with which he spoke, that made every one fall back, and let him take his post of peril, who can tell? Even Nat and Banner stood on one side, watching as he went up nimbly, with his thin hands and naked feet, from round to round of the ladder, his upturned face shining in the lurid light with a strange smile upon it. Haslam saw him too, and stood leaning eagerly at one of the windows to watch his progress, as if too bewildered to see that he could himself reach the ladder by which his son was ascending. The crowd shouted to him, and beckoned; but he leaned upon the window-sill, fascinated and paralyzed.

"God have mercy upon them both!" cried Nat, as Tom was lost to his sight for a moment in the dense smoke from the story below. Just then there was a loud crash heard, and the flooring upon which Haslam stood gave way, and fell into the smouldering fire beneath; while the ladder to which Tom was clinging slipped with the falling in of the window, and the boy was hurled down amongst the crowd below. For the father there was no help or deliverance, even though his son had been willing to give his life for him.

"Make way there!" shouted Banner, pushing his way through the throng, "the lad belongs to me. Oh, Tom! Tom! look up and speak! don't you know me—Banner, and Nat Pendlebury? Look at us, Tom!"

Tom's eyes opened for a moment, and he looked into

Banner's face with a look of mingled agony and contentment. But the instant afterwards he was insensible again, and Banner lifted him up tenderly in his arms, and with Nat making way for him, they passed on through the great gates. As they left the burning mill behind them they met Mr. Worthington and Mr. Hope hurrying to it, and Mr. Hope stopped to speak to them.

"A boy injured!" he said; "was he in the mill? How did he get hurt?"

"It's our Tom," answered Banner, sorrowfully; "Thomas Haslam, sir. His father was in the mill, and he was trying to save him. We're taking him to Pilgrim Street, to Nat Pendlebury's, sir."

"No, no," said Mr. Hope, "you must take him at once to the infirmary. There'll be every care taken of him there, Nat; you must let him go to the infirmary, where there are the best doctors and the best nurses. I'll follow you there presently myself. Lose no time, Banner. Is he much hurt?"

"He fell from a good height," answered Banner; "but he did not fall on the flags,[1]—some of the people caught him. I hope Tom isn't going to die yet awhile. Haslam is dead. He was in the top story, and the floor fell in. It was him that fired the mill, and there's no chance that he's alive. Mr. Hope, I never saw a face look like Tom's when he was trying to save his father!"

By this time a cab had driven up, and Banner, still holding Tom in his arms, took his seat in it, with Nat beside him, and before long they reached the entrance of the infirmary. It is a large pile of buildings, with many windows in it, and in most of them could be seen that soft, subdued light which tells of a room where some malady is being suffered. The illuminated clock in the center of the building showed that it was still half an hour from midnight, only two hours since Tom was talking

1 Flags—a pavement of flat stones.

to Nat at the door of the mill. When Banner bore his sad bur-
den into the entrance hall, he was told that neither the house
surgeon nor the superintendent was gone to bed; and without
any delay Tom was carried into the accident ward, and laid
upon one of the beds which are always in readiness. As Nat
and Banner stood looking sadly upon him, they heard a soft
footfall entering the room, and a lady, with a grave and pitiful
face, approached the bed, and smoothed back the heavy hair, all
singed and scorched by the flames, from Tom's forehead, and
sponged the grime and smoke from his face, until he looked
almost himself again, except that his eyes were closed, and his
lips did not seem to breathe. She spoke to them in a quiet but
clear tone, as though she had long learned to lower her voice to
the key of a sick room.

"You must leave him to us, now," she said; "the house surgeon is coming, but you may stay in the porter's room till you
hear his report. The boy will have every care taken of him. Are
you his father?"

"No, ma'am," answered Nat, to whom she spoke; "but Mr.
Banner here and me love him as if he was our son. We'll be glad
to stay, if you please."

With slow steps, laboring to make no noise, Nat and Banner trode cautiously through the long corridors, on each side of
which there were rooms occupied by sleepless sufferers. They
had to wait a long time, in growing anxiety for the report of the
surgeon. Both of them almost forgot the fire at the mill, in their
intense concern for Tom, except when Banner told the story
of his courage that night to the porter, with a choking voice,
and with tears in his eyes; while Nat, leaning his head upon the
table, sobbed and wept like a child. The report came at last that
no hurt or broken bone could be discovered, but that Tom still
remained in a state of unconsciousness, and that they could not

see him again before the next day, lest they should disturb the other patients in the same ward. So, with heavy and misgiving hearts, Banner and Nat Pendlebury left the infirmary and retraced their steps to the mill.

The fire was still burning, but not with the same fury as when the flooring of the topmost story had given way. The flames were spending themselves, and the engines set to play upon them were gaining steadily, and every quarter of an hour it was evident that the fire was less powerful than before. The crowd of spectators was beginning to thin, as they dropped away one after another to return to their homes, and seek the rest which would be necessary for the labors of the coming day. They were talking one to another of Haslam's fate, and comparing this fire with other fires, pronouncing it to be not as bad as they had expected it to be when the first flame shot up into the midnight sky. Mr. Worthington and Mr. Hope called Nat into the counting-house, and he gave them, his account of the whole night; and they agreed that Haslam's sole motive must have been one of revenge. It was morning before the fire was quite got under, and before the last of the crowd dispersed; and then, with weary steps and a sad face, Nat returned home to his cellar in Pilgrim Street, to make known there the sorrowful events which had happened while Alice and the children had been sleeping peacefully.

Chapter 21

TOM GOES HOME

The morning light was just breaking in the dull east, and the lamps in the infirmary ward were burning dimly, when, with a faint sigh, Tom's consciousness returned. The nurse who was watching beside him saw his eyelids tremble, and his lips move, and when she stooped down to listen, he was murmuring the word, "Father!"

"What is your father's name?" she asked, softly.

"He has no other name," said the boy; "or I've forgotten all the other names."

He spoke with difficulty, and he opened his eyes languidly upon the strange room. It was a long and lofty chamber, with several beds in it, four or five of which were occupied; but the other sufferers had fallen asleep again after the disturbance of his arrival at midnight. It was very still, and the solemn light grew stronger gradually and calmly, with a kind of peacefulness which soothed him, while it slowly awakened his memory. First of all there came to him a sweet and profound feeling that his heavenly Father was regarding him, from moment to moment, with perfect and faithful tenderness, which could never lessen or grow weary; and that Christ, his elder Brother, knew all, and felt all that he suffered, either in body or spirit. These thoughts were so pacifying, that when, very gradually, the events of the past night were allowed to come back to his mind, and, last of all, even the awful moment when, just as he seemed upon the point of saving his father, he found himself falling from the ladder, he was not so shocked and horrified as he must have been had not God so comforted and strengthened him. It seemed almost as if God, to hide it from the boy's heart, placed Himself between the terrible memory and his aching brain; and so, as he lay there, so languid as to be unable to move his head from side to side, yet feeling no pain, the chief thought of his peaceful spirit was of God's infinite love and compassion towards him.

After a while the doctor made his round of the ward, and the soft-voiced and soft-footed nurse came with him to Tom's bedside. He smiled up into their faces with a sweet and strange smile, and the nurse took his hand in hers, and laid her fingers gently upon his pulse.

"Do you feel any pain, my boy?" asked the doctor.

"No, sir," whispered Tom, "no pain at all; I'm very happy."

"Could you get up out of bed and go home?" said the doctor.

Tom's eyes opened widely, and there was a bright light in them, such a look as those eyes sparkle with which have looked upon happy scenes.

"I'm going home," he murmured, "but it is to heaven."

The doctor and the nurse were silent for a minute or two, looking down upon his bright face, from which the gloom and misery of his life of privation and ignorance had quite passed away; and then the nurse spoke in her gentlest and clearest tones.

"Are you sure you should go to heaven if you died?" she asked.

"Ay," said Tom, with more strength; "where else could I go to? When I woke Jesus was saying, 'In My Father's house are many mansions; I go to prepare a place for you.'[1] It is time for me to go home at last."

"No, no," said the doctor, cheerfully, "it is a fancy you've got into your head, my boy. We're going to set you up again here, and turn you out a strong man yet. Where do you feel yourself ill?"

"I don't know," answered Tom, closing his eyes with weariness, "but I feel tired of living; and I think my Father will let me go home. I have no other father now, you know," and his eyes opened again, with the deep glad light in them clouded for a moment; but brightening again as every other thought was lost in the thought of God.

"Is there anything you would like me to do for you?" asked the nurse, bending her ear down again to his lips, for his voice sank into a broken whisper.

"I should like to see little Phil," he murmured, "and Nat Pendlebury, and Alice, and Mr. Banner. Could they come and see me here? They'd be very sorry never to see me again, 'specially little Phil. I'm little Phil's elder brother."

"I will send for them all," answered the nurse, in her clear, distinct tones, which entered into his languid brain easily and soothingly, "and they shall come at three o'clock this afternoon. It is ten o'clock now, and you must keep yourself quiet and go to sleep. The doctor will send you some medicine, and you must take it without giving any trouble."

"No," said Tom, "you're all very good to me, and I've no pain at all. I'm happier than I was at Alderley."

They left him then, and went on to the other beds, but it seemed to Tom as if some one was still beside him, speaking from time to time very softly and gently. He slept perhaps, for the nurse found him with his eyes closed, and his lips just parted

1 John 14:2.

with the feeble breath fluttering between them; but his heart was awake. Never before had it been so wakeful to the thoughts which God's Holy Spirit sought to teach it. It was as if until this time his heart had been heavy, and closed against the sweetest lessons which his heavenly Father had been willing to give to him; but the stone had been rolled away, and his soul had been set free, and now, with a new and trembling delight, he was listening to what God the Lord would say. He was standing like a child at the footstool of his Father, and learning from Him the first syllables of the wisdom which he was to gain during an endless life. It mattered nothing to him that he had had to pass through many troubles and temptations, which every now and then had the mastery over him. They lay all behind him now, passed over and conquered, every one of them having been a step by which he had climbed up nearer and nearer to God; and the lesson he was beginning to learn was to read the history of his own life aright. It was all good—evil as it had seemed while he suffered it; and now he heard a voice saying, a voice which sounded far off and yet was near, "He that overcometh shall inherit all things, and I will be his God, and he shall be My son."

So the hours of the morning glided on; and the nurse came back again and again to his bedside, asking if he were still without pain. He lay motionless, and as it would seem without the power to move; but his answer always was that he felt no pain. Even when the hour of the afternoon drew near when his dear Phil, and Alice, and Nat, and Banner were to come to see him, his profound peace was not broken by any unrest of expectancy. He heard their coming footsteps in the corridor, and his eyes turned towards the door at which they entered, smiling a welcome; but the deep calm of his soul remained untroubled. They gazed upon him with questioning looks. Certainly it was their Tom, with his pinched face, so well known! but who had ever seen a glad light like that which shone in his eyes, or the smile of triumph which lay like sunshine upon his features? Nat and Banner stood still, as if struck dumb with amazement; but Alice sank down on her knees, and laid her face on Tom's hand, while little Phil sprang forward with an exceedingly sorrowful cry, and climbed upon the bed, and pressed his rosy face against Tom's white one.

"Hush thee, Phil!" said Tom, soothingly; "I'm very happy, my little lad, and I feel no pain. Hush thee, Phil!"

"Thee'rt not going to die, Tom!" cried Phil, clinging to him.

"I'm going to heaven!" answered Tom; "why, it's better so a hundred times, Alice, and Mr. Banner, and Nat. If I stayed here I should be nought else but a poor, ignorant, sickly man. I've been a thief, and father was a thief, and when Phil grew up folks would cast it at him; but now it'll be forgotten by the time little Phil is a man. I shall be forgotten, and father, and there'll be nobody to keep Phil back. He'll be a learned man, will Phil, and a good man, please God. I'll tell God all about him. But oh! He knows better than me, and He loves us all better than we love one another."

"Have you no fear of going to be judged by God?" asked Banner, who stood erect at the foot of the bed, keeping down his sorrow with a stern self-command, though he could have knelt down with Alice beside Tom, or, like Nat, have hidden his face in his hands, and sobbed aloud. The other patients were sitting propped up, and listening eagerly to all that was said; for they knew well that Tom must die, and already the shadow or the light from the next life had fallen upon him. The nurse bathed his forehead, and moistened his parched lips, which parted again with a smile, and he opened his eyes, and looked brightly at Banner.

"Why should I be afraid?" he asked, in a tone of gentle

reproval. "He sent His Son into the world to take away our sins, and be our elder Brother. Jesus has taken away all my sins, and I'm not going to judgment. Or, if there is a Judge, and the angels take me to stand before Him, I shall look into His face, and it'll be my Father's face smiling at me. Why should I be afraid?"

"But we're all miserable sinners," said Banner, fearful lest Tom should have a presumptuous confidence in the love of God.

"Ay!" answered Tom, humbly, "but God knows all that I've done. I shan't need to tell Him anything, and yet He is my Father in heaven. I'm glad He knows all about me."

His trembling voice failed him again for a while, and Banner's erect head sank a little, as if he could not long keep his self-control. One or two of the men in the other beds sighed heavily, as they heard Tom say he was glad that God knew all. Phil lifted up his face from the pillow, and looked wistfully into Tom's eyes.

"Tom," he said, "thou'rt not glad to leave me, and Alice, and everybody? Mr. Banner has given thee another cart, and thou'lt not be so poor and starved again. If thou'lt get well, and live till I grow up, we'll have a nice house together somewhere. Oh, Tom, Tom! thee should not wish to die!"

Tom made a great effort to lift up his hand and place it fondly on little Phil's, and his eyes looked lovingly at Alice, and Nat, and Banner. But he could not answer immediately, and when he spoke it was in a very faint yet steady voice.

"If I had everything I could think of," he said, "if we were all rich, and could go and live at Alderley, and never have any more trouble, I'd rather go away, and see God, and hearken to His voice. Oh! little Phil, I love thee dearly, and thee, Alice, and all of ye. I wish ye were all going with me. But I'd rather go to God, I am not unkind towards any one, but He is my Father, and I hanker after seeing His face. I've no other father now."

For the last time there was a tremor and a chill over his peace as he said these last words sadly; but then his voice grew stronger, and his face more joyous, after a moment's silence.

"I haven't words to tell you," he said, "but it seems like as if, could I hearken a little more, I should near Him speak; and there's a light all about me, as if, could my eyes look at it more steadily, I should see His face shining through it. But my eyes'll be dim and my ears dull a little longer. As soon as I can't see you, and hear your voices, I shall see and hear God. I love Him best. Who ought I to love best, save my Father?"

"Oh, Tom, Tom!" cried Banner, sinking down upon his knees, "you know God better than me. It is true what you say, and I believe it now. He is our Father, more than our Judge. I'll not be afraid of Him, and I'll try to be like a little child before Him. I see it all now! I could only love Him a little because I thought He was a strict Judge, and I was fearful of Him; and I myself have been judging people all my life. But I'll love Him more, and love them, because He is the Father! Oh, Tom, my boy, I love you dearly!"

"Ay," murmured Tom, "we needn't be afeard of loving God."

He lay speechless for a while longer, looking from one to another, with eyes that almost spoke the loving words his lips could not utter. The nurse laid her hand softly upon his cold temples, and upon his wrist; and he understood well that his heart was beating slowly towards its last throb. The smile upon his face grew more solemn, but not less happy. Alice was there, and Nat, and Banner, and he was looking upon them for the last time; and little Phil, who had lain nearest to his heart all his life, was closest to him now, hand in hand with him, as the last moment of his earthly hours crept onwards. He stretched out his feeble hand towards them, and they clasped it fondly in their own, one after another, while he whispered, "Good-bye." Then another stillness and silence fell upon them all—not one

of painful sorrow, though it was full of tender regret for the loss
of Tom, until it was broken by a coming footstep, and Tom
opened his eyes once more, though they had been closed as if
the light they looked upon was too bright for them, and he saw
Mr. Hope standing by Banner at his side.

"Little Phil," he whispered, twisting his fingers in Phil's fair
curls for the last time.

"Yes, Tom," said Mr Hope, "I will take charge of little Phil.
He shall be well cared for, my poor boy."

Tom could not speak again for some minutes, but lay still,
gathering up all his strength. Then he lifted up his head a little,
and looked round him eagerly upon the men who, propped up
in their beds, had their faces turned towards him with intent
earnestness, and upon all the dear friends who were watching
with him till he should go beyond their companionship. All
his face was lit up, not so much with a smile, but with some
glory coming whence they knew not; and they could hardly tell
whether it was the pinched and toilworn face they had learned
to love, or the radiant and peaceful face of an angel.

"I didn't know that I had any father save him in jail," he said,
in a clear triumphant tone, "but God is our true Father. The
body dies, and is buried; but if we are born of God we shall live
for ever and for ever. The children of God can never die. I was a
thief, and the son of a thief, but Jesus gave me power to become
one of the sons of God."

His voice faltered as he uttered the last sentence, and the
word God was spoken in a whisper; but so still were they all
that it could be heard like the last sweet sound of some quiet
strain of music, which we hold our breath to hear. The glory
died away softly and gradually from his face, but the peace and
gladness remained, mingled with a solemn awe. Mr. Hope lifted
up little Phil from the bed and carried him away gently in his

arms, while Alice, and Nat, and Banner, bending over the dear face, kissed the cold and silent lips, which still wore the smile with which they murmured the last words, "Jesus has given me power to become one of the sons of God."[1]

---

1 John 1:12.

Chapter 22

PILGRIM PLACE

hen Banner left the ward where Tom's life of poverty and privation had been exchanged for a rich and glorious immortality, he went out into the noisy streets of the city, looking upon every one whom he met, but especially upon the street boys like Tom, with a new and deep interest. He was sad; but the words Tom had spoken were so occupying his brain still that he could not help murmuring to himself, "We needn't be afraid of loving God." He had been influenced, hitherto, chiefly or wholly by the dread of standing at the bar of God, and all his religion had been darkened by the dread of Him as a Judge. When he was about his duty—and he had striven hard to be a conscientious and efficient police officer— he had been constantly engaged in suspecting, and accusing, and arresting wrong-doers, and bringing them to justice, until his heart had been closed against the thought of the compassionate and tender relationship which God is willing to enter into with men, even the chief of sinners. But Tom's words had pierced through all the hardness which had gathered round him, and had placed God before him in a new light. Yes, God was our Father; not only Creator, King, and Judge, but above all and beyond all these our heavenly Father; and every one who would truly hallow His name must know Him by the name of Father. Each one of the wretched and degraded creatures who looked askance at Banner as he passed by, or slunk away out of sight down back streets and narrow slums, might, through the grace of Christ, become a child of God. With what different eyes did he regard them, and how pityingly he began to think of their condition! He marvelled at his own hard exactness when he had pursued them with the rigour of the law, and he said to himself, "They are my brothers and sisters; and they also may become the sons and daughters of the Lord God Almighty."

In one of the pleasant suburbs of Manchester, about two miles from the busy and noisy heart of the city, there is a cemetery, where the din of the streets can be scarcely heard, and where Tom had sometimes been with Nat Pendlebury and the children, walking with them quietly amongst the trees and flowers which are planted round the graves. Here in a sunny place, farthest from the noise of the road which passes by the gates, they buried Tom with many tears, yet thinking of him as having gone to the true home, from which he should go out no more for ever. It was a long way from Pilgrim Street, but as they stood looking down into the open grave, Nat and Alice said to one another that their walk would oftenest be to see that it was kept free from weeds, and that flowers bloomed upon it, as upon many other graves in the pleasant cemetery. They lingered for awhile in the quiet of the place, as if reluctant to leave the spot where their loved Tom was lying; but at last, when the shadows of the coming evening fell, they turned away with a feeling of peaceful sadness, and with slow footsteps went back through the bustling noisy thoroughfares, where no one knew and no one cared either for the sadness or the peace, until they reached their own dark but familiar Pilgrim Street.

"I will turn in with you, Nat," said Banner, who had been one of them at Tom's funeral, and lingered with them beside his grave, and walked leisurely home with them in the twilight. "I feel as if I should be lonesome in my lodgings, and I want to talk with you a bit. You'll let me come in, won't you?"

Would they let him come in! Why, Banner was like a dear old friend to them by this time, and not one of the little ones even was afraid of him. To the folks of the world outside, perhaps, he might seem as stiff and stern as ever, and that was a question in the minds of Alice and Nat; but to them his face was mild and gentle, and his voice the welcome voice of a friend. He might come in and out of their house as he pleased, and never see a cold or frightened look on their faces; and he, feeling sure of that in his inmost heart, stepped in and took a seat in the chimney corner, with little Joey on his knee.

"If only Tom and Phil were here," said Banner, glancing round him, "it would be something like the day we all had tea together, after poor Tom came home, the first time I ever had tea with you, Nat. Will you let me have some tonight?"

Would they! Whether Nat spoke first, or Alice jumped up first to put the kettle on the fire, it would be hard to say. There was still a vague sadness, and sense of something lost, clinging to them; but Banner's appeal to their hospitality recalled them to their usual activity, and Nat bustled about, and helped to set everything in readiness, whilst the water boiled in the kettle. In an incredibly short time the tea was ready, and they sat down to it with grave but pleasant enjoyment. Perhaps they were not quite so long over it as over the feasts made on Phil's holidays, and once or twice Alice had to wipe the tears away from her eyes; but they were not melancholy. Why should they grieve as those who know not what has become of their loved and lost ones?

They gathered round the fire again when tea was over, and

sang one of Tom's favorite hymns, that hymn which he sang to himself as he went home to his father's sordid lodging-room, after the pleasant day at Alderley. Tom's funeral day had brought each one of them also "a day's march nearer home;" and when they came to the last verse they sang the chorus over three or four times, one after another beginning afresh, as if they could not leave off singing Tom's hymn. Then Banner, with Joey again on his knee, looked hard at Nat, and a stern expression, the old stern look, came back to his face.

"I've something to say, Mr. Pendlebury," he said, so severely that Nat sat bolt upright in his chair. "I've been a policeman this fifteen years, and it's been my duty to take people up, and watch 'em, and spy after 'em, and generally to be rather pleased when I caught any of 'em up to mischief; all of which has been very much against me as a Christian man. More than that, I've lived in lodgings, and always been obliged to keep my eye upon my landlady, and be very sharp lest I got cheated; and there's been nothing at home or abroad to keep my heart soft and loving. Before I knew poor Tom, and for a long time afterwards, I was a hard man; and I thought that God Almighty was harder than me, and was always watching for our sins, and reckoning them up, like a miser reckons his gold, as if He took a delight in judging us. Ah! He must judge us, I know; but, if I may so say, it's a grief and trouble to Him, and He has given His only begotten Son to deliver us from His judgments. But the question with me, Mr. Pendlebury, is, How can I keep myself from being so hard?"

Nat was not sitting so upright now, and there was a smile upon his face very pleasant to see, before which Banner's frown quickly vanished away.

"I'm not a scholar," answered Nat, "but I can tell thee how I keep happy and content. I try to think of God, and look up to Him, just like the little ones do to me. Why, bless thee, little Suey knows almost nothing about me, save that I'm her father; she doesn't know my name is Nathaniel Pendlebury, and I'm the watchman at Worthington's mill; and she doesn't know how I get the food she eats, and the clothes she puts on; but she does know I'm father, and loves her dearly. Well, we cannot know much more than that of God till we are grown up in heaven; so, when I begin to feel hard and mistrustful, I look at the little ones, and see how they trust me, and I go and try to do the same towards God."

"I haven't any little ones about me," said Banner, somewhat sadly.

"And then," continued Nat, "if I feel hard against other folks, I think maybe after all they'll go to the same home in the long run, and have the same Father, and it 'ud never do to shut your hearts agen your own brothers and sisters. The children never make me so angry as when they quarrel one with another, and maybe it is the same with Him above."

"Nat," said Banner, after a few minutes of profound thought, "I've had a plan in my head ever since poor Tom died, which would be good for us all, I hope, and would make me a happier man. I've saved a good sum of money, being single and steady, though I say it of myself, and a few weeks ago I bought two cottages up near the cemetery. They are built with a little parlor and a bay-window to the front, and a bit of garden, and a kitchen, and a good scullery behind, and a yard and a drying-ground at the back. Upstairs there are three bedrooms, a little one over the scullery,[1] and the other two a fair size. They are not papered and painted yet, but they soon will be. Now, I'm tired of living in lodgings, and always having my eye on the landlady; and what I wish to propose is this: why shouldn't you and the

1 Scullery—a place where dishes and kettles are kept and cleaned.

children come and live with me in one of my own cottages, and Alice keep house for us all? I should have somebody to care for, and to care for me, and not have everything at home and abroad to keep me a hard man."

Banner's proposal struck Nat with such utter amazement that he could only stare at him for a few minutes, while Banner's face grew red, and his eyebrows were knitted into a heavy frown. But the embarrassing silence was broken by Alice, who clapped her hands together with delight.

"Oh, I should like it!" she cried; "and, Mr Banner, I would try to be the very best housekeeper in Manchester. Father, the children 'ud grow up strong and hearty, better than here. Only Kitty and father 'ud be too far from the mill."

"I've thought of that, Alice," said Banner, smiling again; "Mrs. Worthington and me were talking it over, and she said if Kitty liked she'd take her into her own service, and have her well brought up to be a house servant, and the same with Polly and the others as they grew out of hand. It's better for young girls than the mill, Nat. And you can go down outside the bus for twopence of an evening and morning, if you didn't like the walk. And Phil is to be sent to a real grand school, for Mr. Hope says he is clever enough to learn many things they don't teach at Ardwick. So if you agree to my plan, Nat, I think we shall all be pretty well settled. We shall be near poor Tom's grave—though why I call him poor I don't know—and of evenings the children and me will keep it as neat and pretty as a garden."

Nat looked round him upon the poor cellar where he had lived so long on the window with its little dark panes of dis-colored glass, and the scanty furniture, and the many-colored screen, and the tears sprang to his eyes. The change would be very good and pleasant for the children; but for himself, his feet would often turn towards Pilgrim Street, when they ought to be taking another road to another home. But he was very thankful; and letting the tears dry without wiping them away, lest they should damp the joy of the children, he stretched out his hand, and shook Banner's heartily.

"I can't thank thee," he said, "but some day or other thee will know how much good thee has done me and the little ones. I've been very happy in Pilgrim Street, and I love the very sound of the name. What's the name of the new houses, Mr. Banner?"

"They haven't any name yet," answered Banner; "we couldn't call it a street, because there are only two houses, but we might, if you all liked, call it Pilgrim Place, to keep the old home in your minds. What do you think of it for a name?"

It was agreed unanimously that Pilgrim Place would be the very best name to give the new home. They did not, however, take possession of it until the Lady-Day following; and after all the labor and disorder of settling down was over, little Phil, who was staying for the few days of the Easter holidays at Mrs. Worthington's, was invited to come and see them. When he and Banner approached the cottage, they saw all the children looking out for their arrival, and as soon as they came in sight they sallied forth with shouts of welcome to meet them. It was a fine, mild spring day; and before they went into the house Nat and Alice came out, and locking the door behind them, they bent their steps to the cemetery where Tom's grave was. The trees were covered with purple buds, which would by-and-bye burst into leaf, and there was still a snowdrop or two blossoming amid the turf which covered the grave. They talked together in low but cheerful voices; and Banner kneeling down beside little Suey, the youngest of them all, guided her tiny fingers along the last line carved upon the headstone, while he spelt, letter by letter, these words, "He that overcometh shall inherit all things; and I will be his God, and he shall be My son."

TOM'S GRAVE.

Printed in Great Britain
by Amazon

21768896R00091